T0149375

GUILTY UNTIL PROVEN INNOCENT

GUILTY UNTIL PROVEN INNOCENT

Chumeng Li

iUniverse, Inc.
Bloomington

Guilty Until Proven Innocent

iUniverse books may be ordered through booksellers or by contacting:

iUniverse
1663 Liberty Drive
Bloomington, IN 47403
www.iuniverse.com
1-800-Authors (1-800-288-4677)

Because of the dynamic nature of the Internet, any web addresses or links contained in this book may have changed since publication and may no longer be valid. The views expressed in this work are solely those of the author and do not necessarily reflect the views of the publisher, and the publisher hereby disclaims any responsibility for them.

Any people depicted in stock imagery provided by Thinkstock are models, and such images are being used for illustrative purposes only.
Certain stock imagery © Thinkstock.

ISBN: 978-1-4759-2721-4 (sc)
ISBN: 978-1-4759-2722-1 (ebk)

Printed in the United States of America

iUniverse rev. date: 06/19/2012

Chapter One

"Daniel!" yelled David, "Come hit with me, practice doesn't start until 5:30!"

I shook my head but slowly made my way toward the tennis courts. My dad could not pick me up until later, and I did not want to walk to the town's small library since I did not bring any textbooks to study or do homework from.

James Bake, the tennis coach, was on one of the higher elevated courts, teaching his 3:00 o'clock group of young kids the basics of tennis. Practice on Wednesday started at 5:30, but some players from the high school team, which I used to be part of, started their practice early so they could go home early.

At first I just sat on the bench, which was right next to the tennis court, listening to music and watching them play. Then after a while, I had an irresistible itch to get on the court and play. Since I was not playing for the tennis team this year, I was rusty, and wanted to see if I could still keep up with the people I used to play with.

"David, can I borrow your racket? I just want to hit with Sean for a few minutes," I said.

"Why don't you borrow a racket from James Bake? Doesn't he have a lot of rackets with him all the time?" David said. David was the kid you could not get mad at. His face always had a smile on it, earning him the nickname of Smiley.

"Hmm, well he doesn't like me much ha-ha, and I have not talked to him in a long time. It would just be awkward for me. Could you borrow a racket from him for me? Please."

"Okay, sure. But let me use my racket and you use his," said David.

"Yeah, okay."

While David ran to the upper courts to borrow a racket from James Bake, I hit with Sean a couple times. The first point was pretty long, so I decided to go for an all or nothing shot, smashing it as hard as I could to the left corner. It was a perfect shot.

"Oh my God! Daniel's still got it! Okay, okay, I see how it is," Sean chuckled as he fed me another ball to start another point.

This time, I tried essentially the same thing, but hit it so far out that it flew into the fence before landing. David had returned, so we switched rackets.

For about thirty minutes, I played with friends who were on the team like George, Sean, and David. It seemed like most people still opted for the original practice that started at 5:30. But by then, it began to get really cold. Other team members began to show up and play as well. Just as I was about to leave, Fred Guo, a former team #1 who had not practiced and dropped in the rankings, arrived. I had not talked to Fred in over a year, though we used to be close, so I walked to my original spot on the bench and sat there shivering. On the court closest to me, Christopher and Bill were playing against Sean. I stood up and jumped around a bit to keep warm. I looked at the trash can to my right, and saw a really big gadget on it. It was definitely not an iPod though it had the white iPod ear buds attached to it.

I walked over to it, and picked it up.

"Hey Christopher!" I yelled, "Is this phone yours?" In my head I thought, it had to be either his or Bill's because they took Web Development and they always attended conferences where they would receive high tech stuff like this. If it was one of theirs, I would ask to play with it for awhile.

"No it's not," Christopher said as he glanced up for a second.

"Bill? Is this your phone?"

"Nope."

I put the phone down. Stupid place to leave such a nice phone, I thought.

Seconds after I put the phone back on the trash can, George walked over and pocketed it.

"Is that your phone? When did you get a new one?" I asked.

"It's Fred's, he's pissing me off," George said.

"What's he doing?"

"He keeps doing that barf-bag stuff every time I hit the ball. Like it isn't that bad of an insult, but it's so annoying."

"You're really going to steal it straight up like this?" I asked.

"Yeah," George said, as he began to pack up quickly.

"Are you leaving now?" I asked him.

"Yup, it's way too cold to play right now, and it's so windy."

"All right, I'll leave with you."

We walked off the courts and began to walk around the grass field that encompassed the tennis courts.

"You sure you want to do this?" I asked again.

"Hmm you're right," George said. He leaned through the fence and yelled, "David! Come over here."

"Yeah?" David said.

"Here, take this phone," George said as he slipped Fred's phone through an opening in the fence, "When Fred gets nervous and asks about where his phone is, give it back to him. But not before."

"Why?" asked David.

"Just do it," said George, "He's pissing me off, so I just want to get him back a little bit."

"No, get someone else to do it. Why can't Christopher do it?" David asked.

"Wow, it's not a big deal," George said.

"What if Fred gets mad at me and says I stole it?"

"Tell him I gave it to you then. Besides, it's not even stealing if you give it right back like twenty seconds afterward. It's just a joke," George said.

"Fine," said David, "wait, can I put it somewhere else? Like instead of holding onto it, can I just put it somewhere else so I don't get in trouble."

"Sure, sure whatever," George said.

George walked over to unlock his bike from the bike rack as I waited. Then we headed toward the town library together.

AFTER I GOT home that night I had totally forgotten about what happened at the tennis courts. I sat down at my desk and began to do some homework. I put my phone down next to my laptop; it barely touched my desk before it started to ring.

I looked down at it, and it said that Josh was calling me. That's weird, I thought.

"Hello?" I answered.

"Daniel, where the hell is my phone?!" yelled a voice.

"Who is this?" I asked.

"It's Fred. I know you took my phone. Give it back to me right now."

"Um, I didn't take your phone Fred," I said.

"Yea you did, don't fucking lie to me," he cursed.

"I didn't even take it. Why are you yelling?"

"Then who the hell has it?" he asked.

"George took it and gave it to David," I said.

I could hear Fred yell, "David? Do you have my phone?!"

There was a brief pause.

"David says he doesn't have it," Fred said to me after questioning David, "You better bring me my phone tomorrow. I'm going to call George now, but if I don't get my phone back you're going to get your ass kicked. And so will George. Do you want to get your ass kicked?"

"Look," I started, but realized that Fred had hung up.

What was that? I got heated and angry, I wanted to call back to yell and cuss at Fred, but then my parents would hear me so instead, I logged onto my Facebook account to set my status.

What would adequately describe my anger? I thought. After fiddling with a few decisions, I landed on, *Fred Guo, Stupid Ass Bitch.*

Fred wasn't added as my friend on Facebook so I knew he wouldn't be able to see my status.

Thursday, April 1ˢᵗ

I arrived at school on Thursday with no thoughts about what had happened the previous night. I sat through a pretty boring math class, a difficult Spanish class, and an entertaining English class before finally having the opportunity to eat something since I was starving.

I walked with Nathan downstairs to the gym lobby of the school and met up with George and Robert. After a few minutes of deliberation, we chose to go to Zari's Deli to get some sandwiches. It was a Thursday, and I had no more classes after lunch. George, Robert, Nathan and I walked past the old tiny houses on Locklear Boulevard, turned onto Tamarac Avenue and walked into Zari's. Normally there was always a line of twenty-five people, but to our surprise there was no line. We bought lunch and walked back to the school, where a bunch of people were playing basketball. The basketball team rarely ever played during lunch, so sometimes the people on the court would make a silly mistake that everyone saw would laugh at. We sat there munching on our sandwiches and watching the basketball game. All of a sudden Fred walked up to George, who sat on the left of Robert who was on my left.

"George! Give me back my headphones," Fred yelled.

"All right, here," George said as he handed Fred's white iPod headphones back to Fred.

Fred held them up and examined them for a few seconds before saying, "These aren't mine. Where are my headphones George?"

"How are those not yours? Those are your headphones," George said.

"No they aren't, how are you going to prove it?"

"I can't, but those are yours. What do you want me to do?"

"You swear these are mine?" Fred asked.

"Yes."

"Swear on your mother's life," Fred continued.

"No I'm not going to do that."

"Then that means you're lying to me. Come on George, swear on your mother's life that these are my headphones."

"Fine, whatever. Sure," George said.

"Okay, if I prove these aren't my headphones, than I'm going to kill your mom."

"Wow, Fred, shut up. Get out of here. What makes you think you can talk to people like that?" I said.

"You have a problem with me Daniel? You have something you wanna say to me?" Fred said as he walked in front of me, looking down at me as he stood there holding the headphones he claimed were not his.

"Not really. Just get out of here." I said.

"Why should I?" Fred asked.

"Why are you talking to people like that? George gave you your headphones back, so you shouldn't be threatening to kill his mom or making him swear on his mother's life." I said.

"Oh yea? Do you want to fight?"

"Just leave," I said and looked at Nathan, who was to my right, and just shrugged.

"Daniel, did you know that there are no cameras around here?" Fred said as he took a look around, "It's not like the hallways where there are cameras everywhere.

I could bitch-slap you right now, and no one would know."

I looked at him again. This time he faked a punch to my face, causing me to flinch. I stood up, so that I looked down on him, and so I could defend myself if he actually did hit me.

Fred began to yell at me, "Daniel, you have no friends . . . No one wants to talk to you . . . Why don't you get out of here . . ."

I tuned him out. He was yelling at the top of his lungs and I did not care about what he had to say to me. I tried being reasonable and looked at Nathan, who was sitting down next to me and said, "Hey Nathan," I said with a slight grin, "You know that quote where someone said, 'don't argue with fools because people from a distance can't tell who is who'?"

As I watched a smile form on Nathan's face, I felt something hit my head, right on my left ear.

I turned around to see Fred walking away at a brisk pace.

"Wow! Really dude?!" Nathan yelled.

"Oh my god, he has issues," George said.

"Hey Robert," I said, "How much time is there left for lunch?"

"Um, seven minutes."

"Alright, let's go to Mrs. Bush's office. I need some witnesses."

"Do I have to go dude?" Nathan said, "what if I just come down when they call down and be a witness?"

"Sure," I said, "But George, you have to come."

"Hey, I'm going to be a witness too," Robert said.

"Okay, yeah," George said.

George and I walked to the attendance office where Mrs. Bush's office is located in and asked the secretary to see Mrs. Bush.

We were told that Mrs. Bush was out on lunch duty watching the kids, and that she shouldn't be far from the front entrance of the school. We went outside to see that she was right there, and started to talk to her. When she realized that it was a serious matter, she led us inside. As George and I explained what had happened throughout lunch, the bell rang and all the students either began to the dreaded walk to their classes. George and I however, were headed for the attendance office.

First, Mrs. Bush asked us if there were any witnesses. Then we sat at a desk to write down what had occurred. As we wrote, Robert, Nathan, and Christopher were called down into Mrs. Bush's office one by one.

George and I sat in the reception area of the office silently, waiting to be excused back to our sixth period class. However, neither of us was excused. Seventh period began, and we were called into Bush's office one by one.

The office was about twelve feet by ten feet. The door was located on the left side of the office so that if you walked in, the only direction you could turn and walk was right. There was a large, standard teacher's desk with a chair behind it for Mrs. Bush and two chairs across from it for people like me who were called down to talk to her. On the walls, she hung up Chester High School Banners and banners of universities I had never heard of. I had been in this office before, and normally the results of the meetings in this office didn't favor me much.

"So explain to me what happened. I think I get the gist of it already though," Mrs. Bush began.

I explained what happened again, basically repeating what I had said and she sat there listening and taking notes the whole time. Occasionally, she nodded and smiled but for the most part she held a serious mood.

"Why was he so mad at you?" She asked.

"I don't know. He was not my friend and we had not talked to each other for long time except yesterday evening," I answered.

"What happened yesterday evening?"

"He called me and accused me of taking his cell phone. I told him I didn't, and George gave the phone to David. He said he would call George and said some nasty stuff." I did not repeat exactly what Fred said.

"How could he call you if he could not find his phone?" She asked.

"He used Josh's phone."

"Josh?"

"Josh Hsu."

"Hsu?"

"Yes, H S U."

"Okay. I think you already told me when happened during lunch time today. He slapped you? And you didn't hit him back?"

"Well I didn't see him slap me because I was looking away from him, and when I turned around he had already walked off," I answered.

"So it was a slap, and not a punch?" Mrs. Bush asked.

"Yeah, he slapped me right here above my left ear," I said and turned my head slightly.

"Oh yeah. Your ear is red. So it's pretty obvious that he hit you, and pretty hard too would you say?"

"No, not that hard, but it definitely wasn't a playful, messing around kind of slap. There was some ill-intent behind it," I answered.

"Okay, here will you turn you head to the right and I'm going to take a picture of your left ear as evidence. And also one of your right ear just to show the difference." Said Mrs. Bush.

"Okay,"

"Yes. Alright Daniel, thanks for reporting it to me and not fighting back. I know that's a hard thing to do but you did the right thing. You're excused; do you need me to write you a pass back to class?"

"No I don't have a seventh period."

"Okay then, do you want some ice for your ear? It's definitely red and it looks a little bit swollen," she offered.

"No it's okay, it's not hurting that much. My ear just feels a little warm though, I'm fine," I said.

"Okay, when you go out can you get George in here as well?"

"Yeah," I said and walked out.

Friday, April 2<u>nd</u>

I felt pretty good about myself. Instead of losing my temper and going back to fight Fred for slapping me for what I believed to be a silly reason, I handled it the way the school officials said to handle it.

"Daniel!" said Mr. Edwards, "Here's a note for you."

"Do I go now? Oh, end of the period. Okay, thanks," I said.

I turned to Nathan, "Crap, why can't this be over with."

"You got to go down to Bush's office again? Damn," said Nathan.

"I wonder what's going to happen."

After the bell rang signaling the end of the school day, I made my way down the stairs slowly with Nathan joking and talking the whole time. We walked into the Gym Lobby area of the school and talked for a couple more minutes until Nathan reminded me that I had to go to Bush's office. Reluctantly, I walked over there.

"Hey dude!" George called from behind me, "Are you going to Bush's office right now?"

"Yeah, did you already go in there?" I asked.

"Yep, it's so bullshit dude. She told me I'm getting suspended for one day for behavior leading up to a fight," George said.

"What behavior? You weren't even in the fight. And it wasn't even a fight," I said.

"I don't know. I think it has something to do with the headphones. And how I took his phone. Dammit this is such bullshit!" George said.

We reached the door to the attendance office.

"I do not want to go in there," I said.

"Just get it over with," George said.

"You still coming in?"

"Yeah, I have to."

I wondered what was going to happen to me. George was a victim of verbal abuse and got suspended. I too was a victim of the situation, but if George's behavior led up to a fight then mine must have. There is no way I'm going to get suspended for this, I thought. George took his phone and headphones but gave them back, I didn't do anything.

"Daniel! Come on in," Mrs. Bush

George looked at me and shrugged and I kind of rolled my eyes before I walked into Ms. Bush's office. I looked down at my watch, it was about 2:25pm.

"Have a seat. How are you today?" asked Mrs. Bush.

"Fine," I answered.

"So you came in here yesterday to report to me that you were slapped by Fred during lunch time yesterday which is 100% the right thing to do. You were a victim of that particular situation although you are not faultless would you agree?" she began.

"I guess," I said.

"So Fred has been suspended for an amount of days I cannot reveal to you. He admitted to hitting you so it's automatic that he is suspended. However, upon further investigating, we've found evidence of your behavior that is not acceptable." Said Mrs. Bush.

I began to get worried. What did I do that was so unacceptable and why was it important to bring up right now?

She pulled out some Facebook screenshots of what I could tell was my last status insulting Fred and another one of a photo of what seemed like the tennis team.

"Here are some of the pieces of evidence that indicate that you have been bullying Fred on Facebook, which is cyberbullying. Here is a status you put on facebook calling Fred some dirty words, and then you and George had a back and forth, taking turns saying nasty things about Fred. And on this tennis team photo you used a homophobic slur against him. So it seems like you have a pattern of cyberbullying Fred."

"Okay," I said confidently, "first of all, this all happened outside of school and off school grounds so the school has no jurisdiction to punish me for what I do on Facebook."

"No," she simply stated.

"No what?" I said, "Second of all, I don't even have Fred added as a 'friend' on Facebook so I can't even communicate with him on Facebook at all. Also, I don't talk to him at school at all. How am I supposed to cyberbully him?"

Mrs. Bush looked at me with doubt and squinted her eyes but said nothing.

She then pushed the two screenshots toward me. The date of my status was March 31, 2010 and the date when of my comment on the picture was March 2, 2009.

"Do you realize that these two posts are over a year apart? So this counts as a pattern of bullying to you?" I could not believe it. The posts were thirteen months apart and the school had come to the conclusion that I had a pattern of cyberbullying Fred. "Do you really think that two things I say a year apart is a pattern?"

"Yeah, I have also interviewed about ten students come in here and some of them have confirmed that you have bullied Fred in person as well."

"I haven't talked to Fred in a year! Are you kidding me?" I just about jumped out of my seat. The arguments she presented against me seemed ridiculous. I hadn't talked to Fred since the beginning of the tennis season of sophomore year. "Also," I continued, "Fred called me on Wednesday night, probably five minutes before I posted this status with Josh's phone and said much worse things to me and threatened me. This status is just a reaction. If both people are cussing at each other then it's not bullying."

"Look, calm down. It doesn't matter what you say anymore. The decision has been made and you are suspended for two days for behavior leading up to a fight."

I really lost it now, they already suspended me, so what did it matter if I kept jawing with her and just get my emotions out.

"Behavior leading up to a fight? There was no fight, as you know. He hit me and I didn't hit back, that is not a fight. What is a fight to you? I can't believe this," I half yelled half said.

"I have enough evidence to think that you were involved in provoking Fred and therefore you were part of a fight."

"No, it doesn't matter what I say to him, he can't hit me. You guys have been telling us that since kindergarten and first grade that no matter what people say you can't use your hands to try and hurt them. So now the rule has changed? When did this happen?" I asked.

"It has never changed. I guess you just never read the rules carefully enough," she said.

"Okay, are these Facebook posts some of the evidence that you have to indicate I started a fight yesterday?" I asked.

"They could be."

"Well, then now you're being ridiculous. The comment on this picture," I said pointing to a picture of the entire tennis team, "was made over a year ago. It was so long ago that I even forgot I had made this comment. Can you really make the connection that our so called fight started a year later because of this?"

"You used homophobic slurs in that photo. I'm not sure why it wasn't reported earlier," she said.

"If you suspended everyone in the school for calling someone gay you would have 99% of the student body in your office right now," I said.

"But they do not have a pattern of bullying like you do," she said, "You repeatedly post cruel things toward Fred on Facebook."

"Calling someone gay is no different from calling someone a man or a woman," I said, "What if I used that defense? Read it again, I didn't say being gay was bad or anything did I?"

"That's not important. I'm not here to discuss ethics with you right now," said Mrs. Bush.

"And, this status calling him a stupid ass bitch was a reaction to a phone call he made toward me that I didn't particularly like," I said.

Mrs. Bush shrugged.

"What's that supposed to mean? It was a reaction, meaning he did something to me first and then I reacted. Maybe it wasn't the nicest reaction in the world, but I didn't start it," I said.

"You've already told me that," she said.

"And knowing that doesn't change your ruling on it at all? You think reacting to a threatening phone call is essentially the same as just straight up calling someone names?" I asked.

"I never said that," she said, "How are we supposed to know if the phone call happened or not?"

"Why do you have such a hard time believing anything I'm saying yet seem so willing to believe all your witnesses that say bad things about me to help Fred out?" I accused.

"I'm not having a hard time believing you. I had ten people's stories who didn't line up with yours."

"Which ten people are you talking about?" I asked.

"By law, I cannot share that with you," she said.

I let out a big breath realizing how I was wasting my efforts trying to make my case at this point.

"Also Daniel, I wasn't done presenting evidence when you started yelling at me. Here are some screenshots of you cyberbullying Harrison Oh," she said and pulled out two more screenshots. One was a screenshot of a photo of Harrison and another was a screenshot of an argument I had via comments with Harrison.

I pointed at the screenshot of my argument with Harrison, "Can I see that, because I have reason to believe that this piece of evidence was tampered with."

"No Daniel. California State Law says that I don't have to show you any of this," she said.

"Okay, if I bring in evidence tomorrow to show that the evidence was manipulated to make me look worse. What if I did that?" I asked.

"You are free to do that, but you are still suspended for cyberbullying Harrison and Fred."

"I didn't even cyberbully Harrison. If you looked at real evidence and all the evidence, you would realize that I didn't start any of this with Harrison and I don't even talk to Fred," I said.

"Is it true that you also made a group on Facebook called the Harrison Fan Club?" she asked.

"Yes," I said, "and now being a fan of someone and making a nice group is against the rules too?"

"I think we can all tell that this is not a sincere group and it is just based off of sarcasm and you're making fun of him."

"Look at this photo, again you use homophobic slurs," she said.

It was a picture of Harrison eating a large lollipop that I had added to the group with the caption, *I lick him like a lollipop.*

"How is this homophobic at all? How do you even know what it even means?" I asked.

"Come on Daniel," she said as she rolled her eyes.

"Did I say Harrison licks him like a lollipop? No it says 'I'. Half of the evidence you present against me is invalid and half of it is off assumption," I said, "Why are you trying so hard to get me suspended. It seems like that."

"I have enough evidence to show that you have cyberbullied Harrison and Fred on a consistent basis and there's nothing you can do about it. If you don't like my decision go talk to Mr. Fahge about it!" she said with her eyes bulging.

"But is your evidence even valid? All the Facebook evidence you have against me is invalid because—"

"It is valid. You cyberbullied another person." She cut me off.

"Outside of school grounds and not during school hours. You have zero jurisdiction to discipline me for what I do outside of school," I argued.

"California has a new state law regarding cyberbullying and I have it printed out right here," she said as she pushed a couple pieces of paper across her desk to me, "I want you to read it and tell me what it says. Then you decided whether or not you cyberbullied them."

"I'm not going to read this," I said, "Facebook apparently had no problem with me saying these things. I never got called by the police for my actions on Facebook but you guys found something so wrong with what I'm doing that it must be against the law right?"

Mrs. Bush leaned back in her chair again, sighed, and shook her head.

"So why don't you leave it up to the police to punish me if it's such a terrible crime I committed? Most of these things having nothing to do with school and also took place outside of the school campus and off school hours."

"Look at it Daniel, it's in the school. We're in Chester High School right now and this evidence is in my hands. It is in school Daniel," Mrs. Bush leaned back in her chair.

"Are you kidding me? The action happened outside of school. Facebook is blocked in school anyways so whoever got those screenshots definitely got them outside of school. Also these incidents have nothing to do with school either," I said as I watched Mrs. Bush roll her eyes and exhale sharply.

"Well," she stuttered, "This photo is a school event at another school and you commented on it too," she said as she pointed at the picture of the tennis team.

"But the comment has nothing to do with school. Only the picture has to do with school and I'm obviously not doing anything wrong in the picture," I said.

"You used homophobic slurs against Fred and Harrison, don't you at least have some creativity?" she challenged.

"Calling someone gay is not homophobic," I stated plainly.

"In the fashion you did it is," she countered.

"No, what did I say? I said that whoever has their legs crossed is gay. That's no different from saying whoever has their legs crossed is a man or whoever has their legs crossed has brown eyes. It is definitely not homophobic. I didn't say being gay was bad or wrong did I?"

"The tone that you said it in for this picture is a homophobic use of the language. Okay, now California passed new laws last year, here are the new laws, I want you to read them." She said as she handed me two pieces of paper stapled together.

"I'm not going to read that. It doesn't apply to me. I didn't bully anybody."

"Well, from my judgment you did," Mrs. Bush said.

"Have you heard of Formspring?" I asked.

"Yes, and there has been speculation of you doing some things on other people's formsprings. Have you?"

"Now you're accusing me of Formspring?"

"No I didn't which is why I didn't bring it up," she said.

"Okay, so what about all those people who say worse things on there than I've said on Facebook?"

"We have no way of knowing who it is," she said, "But there was something that you appeared to have written about your tennis coach, James Bake, on urbandictionary. com."

"What?"

"There's a definition of your name, followed with a sentence that is derogatory toward James Bake. We have some people saying that you posted this. If that's the case than it could be worse for you."

"I have no idea what you're talking about," I said.

"Okay," said Mrs. Bush skeptically.

"I understand that maybe I can't look at this situation from on objective point of view, but you should because it has nothing to do with you. And to me you are really favoring Fred," I said.

"How it is favoring? I have all this evidence here for proof," she scoffed.

"Some of the proof is irrelevant, some of it is fake. What does Harrison have to do with situation, yet you throw that whole thing in here to help punish me and lengthen my sentence probably."

"I have other evidence as well. This thing on twitter you put, 'gunna jack my Chinese ass some more headphones' this is some pretty convincing evidence that you were going to attempt to steal Fred's headphones," she said.

"I haven't been on Twitter account in months! I even forgot I had one until you just said that. Can you please look at the date of that post and then look at the date today. I promise you that if you do, you will understand that some of this evidence you're using doesn't have anything to do with what we're addressing today," I said, "I posted that on Twitter last July right. That's nine months ago. You think I planned all this out nine months in advance?"

"I don't know did you?" she said.

There was a moment of silence where I just glared at her. I really couldn't believe that she really believed what she was saying.

"You can't be serious. All right, where can I appeal this suspension because this, this is just ridiculous," I said.

"You can talk to Mr. Fahge if you want. But he already reviewed and agreed. Look, I have to talk to George now. You've been in here arguing for too long," Mrs. Bush said.

I stormed out of her office.

I didn't know how to feel coming out of that meeting with Mrs. Bush. I had occasionally seen her in the hallways but had little prior interaction with her. From what I knew, she was generally nice but sometimes had a mean streak.

ONE OF MY earlier interactions with Mrs. Bush was during a period of Standardized Testing. This is where I got my general feel for what she is like as a person and as an administrator.

California schools were required to participate in STAR tests, the test that measures students' general knowledge in reading, writing, math, and science. STAR Testing week was always tedious, many students finished the day's testing in half the time allotted, leaving them with about an hour where they are confined to a desk. Teachers also hated the STAR Test but recognized its importance. However, our school had more teachers than classrooms thus allowing many teachers to go take shifts in proctoring the test.

On the second day of testing in my freshman year, Mrs. Bush came into the classroom I was testing in and proctored the math portion of the test. For many students, the math portion is the easiest on the test. We were given two hours to complete forty-five questions and one student, Tim Choi, finished with about an hour left to go. He was one of the last to finish.

Tim took out his iPod and began listening to music. He was minding his own business and not bothering the few people still taking the test. Fifteen minutes later, every single person in the room was done with the test. Mrs. Bush left the room for a moment, and Tim, being the goofball that he was, turned up his music louder and began to sing and dance to the music. As he was in the middle of one little hilarious routine, Mrs. Bush walked back into the room with coffee and a donut.

She did not seem to be pleased at all with Tim's behavior and summoned him to the front of the classroom.

"How old are we now Tim?"

"Fifteen," Tim replied.

"And where are we Tim?" she asked.

"At school?"

"And what are we doing at school?" she asked, this time with a mocking tone.

"Taking the STAR test."

"All right, and you have been taking this test for a long time, you should know that the behavior you just displayed is not acceptable," she said.

"Sorry," Tim mumbled.

"I have to cancel your score for this portion of the test, and you will have to use the extra advisory period to make it up." She said as she bit into her donut.

"But everybody in the room was done with their test! I wasn't distracting anybody—,"

"I don't care," she growled between bites of her donut, "what you did was against the rules and I am to follow protocol. Go bring me your test book and answer sheet."

Tim walked slowly from the front of the classroom back to the desk he was sitting at. He reluctantly picked up his test booklet and answer sheet one by one and walked back to the front of the classroom even slower.

Mrs. Bush was licking the sticky chocolate off her fingers from the donut and grabbed the test booklet and answer sheet. Her thumb left a huge chocolate stain on the test booklet. Tim walked back to his desk but before he even sat down, Mrs. Bush called him back to the front of the room.

"Tim, I've had a change of heart. I'll let you off the hook for this one, but you can't do the same thing again tomorrow! I probably won't be your proctor tomorrow so if you pull the shenanigans you did today, your proctor might actually cancel your scores." With that, Mrs. Bush handed Tim his chocolate covered test booklet and answer sheet.

Everyone in the classroom had gone quiet watching this little encounter unfold and as soon as Tim sat down, everyone resumed what they had been doing. Some were doing homework and some had put headphones on and gone to sleep. There was still about fifty minutes left before the testing period was over and the hallways began to get a little noisy. All of a sudden, some low, husky, giggling broke out near the front of the classroom.

Mrs. Bush had her feet on the desk and was apparently watching something funny on the internet. Something so funny that she apparently could not control her laughter. She had a little bit of chocolate on her face that was smudged there from the donut and that little chocolate mark became bigger and more noticeable as she stretched out her face and laughed. Everybody else had seen her treatment of Tim and remained absolutely quiet, but here she was watching something on the internet and laughing out loud.

AS SOON AS George and I were let go we went to the gym lobby again to talk about what had just happened. Soon afterward, the school bell rang, and all the students who had class walked all around us. A few of our friends came up to ask about what happened.

Nathan was one of the first to ask. After George and I each gave a shortened version of our conversations with Mrs. Bush, all Nathan could manage to say was a long drawn-out "Wow" while tilting his head backward in disbelief.

Somehow, word had gotten out about my suspension as well as George's. People didn't know the whole story, as a matter of fact, neither did I. I had no idea how they connected all of the dots they did to gather enough evidence to suspend me. It was like they took every sin I had committed in a two year period, drew lines between them, and made it seem like everything I've done for two years led to my "fight" with Fred.

More and more people came up to ask me what happened or at least to ask me for details since most knew the basic information already. Most people had looks of disability and the "are you kidding me" laugh with a shaking of their head. Some people got angry and some jokingly suggested that we do something to get back at the school or plan something to frame Fred.

Robin Chen, a senior on the tennis team was one of the first to ask. I didn't feel like putting the effort to tell any details so I only told him my punishment and what I did for the school to give me such a punishment. Robin, a somewhat gullible guy who is known to fall for jokes easily, muttered, "Don't mess with me ha-ha. That's impossible."

This caused just about everyone there to crack a grin. We then had to show Robin the hall passes we got to go down to Mrs. Bush's office. He finally believed us and had a totally different reaction. He brought his palm to his forehead and asked, "What the hell is wrong with them?"

Of course, nobody had an answer. Some of the more outspoken people in the group started spraying their thoughts, "that's some bullshit dude, it's so dumb that you guys are getting punished for some insecure ass sensitive idiot bitching to the school. Dude everyone should be suspended then . . . I call people bitch all the time! On Facebook. Everywhere!"

I appreciated the support and didn't expect anything different from them but it wasn't really making me feel much better.

After about thirty minutes of just talking to friends about it, I got a phone call from my dad, who was on his way to pick me up. He had already learned of my suspension, and was not happy about it. I tried to tell him what happened and why the punishment was not fair, but obviously he was not convinced. I told him that I was going to appeal it, and needed to talk to the principal. He told me to go find the principle now and not wait until after the suspension to appeal.

As I hung up the phone with my dad, I saw Mr. Fahge talking to a school custodian only about thirty feet away from me. I approached him and said gently, "Mr. Fahge can I speak with you?"

"Are you Daniel?" he said nicely, "Yes I heard about what happened. What do you need?"

"Mrs. Bush told me that if I wanted to appeal my suspension that I should come talk to you. I feel—" I said, starting to give reasons why I was appealing.

"Okay, well hold on a second. I can't listen to your whole appeal right now. Our process is that you must serve out the one day suspension, that cannot be changed, and then you can email me with evidence or reasoning on why you feel that the suspension is unfair. I will definitely take time to look over what you have to say and make decisions from there," he explained.

"Wait, Mrs. Bush told me I was suspended for two days."

"Oh, it's two days now. Well when you come back on Wednesday then. Hopefully I will have received an email from you by then and we can talk about it from there," he said.

I could not understand why he could not listen to my appeal now and felt he was playing delay tactic.

"Mrs. Bush told me you already reviewed and approved the suspension. Will my appeal would have any effect?" I asked.

"Well, I do believe in due process and I've yet to see all the evidence, but if you email me I will consider your argument".

"So there's nothing I can do right now to appeal or anything?" I asked.

"That's correct. I am off duty right now and so are most of the school officials," he said.

At that point, my dad called again to ask if I had spoken with the principal yet. I told him that I just spoke with the principal and that I was told I could only appeal the suspension afterward. He asked to speak to the principle. So I had to muster my courage again to approach the principal.

"Mr. Fahge, my dad would like to speak to you."

Mr. Fahge took my cell phone and stated talk to my dad. He pretty told my dad the same thing. Apparently my dad told Mr. Fahge that he was on the way to school and would like to talk to him in person. He also told my dad he did not have time and did not know all the details so there was no reason to meet now. Only Mrs.

Bush had all the evidence and details, but she was not available now.

But he was no more successful than I was and got the same exact words spoken to him from the principal that I did.

How could you approve a suspension without reviewing all the evidences? As I was wondering along the road in front of the school without any purpose, feeling betrayed and frustrated, my dad arrived on the spot. I climbed into the car without even saying a Hi to my dad.

The car ride home wasn't very great. My dad was upset that I did such a stupid thing, and repeatedly asked me what really happened.

"Why did you ask me again and again? I already told you what happened." I said while my eyes stare on the window.

"Because what you told me does not make sense. If George took Fred's phone, why did he hit you and not George? Why did you get suspended if you were a victim?"

"Don't ask me again if you don't believe me!" I yelled and turned my head. For a split of a second I made an eye contact with my dad in the review mirror. Both of us sensed the surprise on the other end, and I fell silent. In my memory I had never yelled at my dad before.

After stop the car in the garage, my dad turned his head and said "I want you to write down what happened, try to include every detail."

"Okay." I mumbled.

Chapter Two

Tennis Tryouts

I first met Fred in seventh grade. He was my classmate in math, English, and history. We weren't close friends but we got along fine.

I didn't have any classes with him in eighth grade, so our friendship never blossomed until Freshmen year tennis tryouts. He was one of the top players, and seemed very friendly as he offered up advice to me and even gave me an over grip to put on my racket handle.

It was the second day of tryouts after a not so great first day. When I set my stuff down by the courts and got my racket out, Fred, who was standing next to me, began to look at my racket.

"Hey, can I see your racket Daniel?"

"Yeah."

"Do you like it? I've never bought a Prince racket before but this one looks like it's good."

"I like it. I mean, it's a lot better than the rackets I used to play with."

"Oh, well I'm thinking about getting a new racket for this season. This N-code I'm using is like three years old."

"Your grip looks like it's really new," I said.

"Oh, I just put on a new over grip today. Watch, by the end of today it'll be grayish again."

"Over grip? Is what I have an over grip?"

"No, yours is just the grip that came with the racket right. You didn't put another grip on it right?"

"Yea, it came like this."

"Oh, well it's kind of slippery now. And yea, it's not an over grip."

"I'm used to how this feels."

"Here feel my grip."

I took his racket and held the racket as if I was going to hit a serve.

"I like it. Where did you get this?"

"I ordered mine online. But you can get them from Plaza Tennis. Here, you can have one of mine."

Fred reached into his bag and took out an over grip. It was packed into a small roll about one inch by one inch.

"Want me to put it on for you?" He asked me.

"No it's okay. You don't have to give me one. I'll go buy some myself."

"It'll help you play better. It's okay, you can have one."

He put the grip on my racket slowly and carefully. Then he handed it to me and said, "See how it feels."

"Wow, thanks dude."

"No problem."

It was already three o'clock and the coach had yet to arrive, so I began to chat with Fred. I had talked to him before but had no idea that he was this good at tennis. I soon found out that he had been playing tennis for five years, taking private lessons once a week. He also played tournaments against other players of similar ages in Northern California. The coach arrived and we ended the conversation.

THE NEXT DAY, Fred, who was ranked #3 on the team, challenged me to a challenge match. Challenge matches were short tie breakers to seven to determine spots on the team. Fred had been playing for a lot longer and therefore was a much better player, but I put up as good a fight as I could.

Fred won the toss and decided to serve first. He only got one serve, and won his point. After I lost the next two points on my serve, I felt a little bit desperate, and started going for bigger shots and won the next two points on his serve by going to net. Whenever I hit good shot, he would often clap by tapping his left wrist to the strings of his racket which he held in his right hand. In the end though, he was just much better than me and won 7-5

"Hey Daniel, you're good enough to play USTA tournaments," He said to me while we were taking a break.

"Yeah, I wanted to do something like that. Is that what the rankings are like?"

"Yep, so if you play and win a lot of tournaments, you get ranked higher and higher. I think you're good enough to play. It helps a lot with tennis and it's really fun," he said.

"Okay, well, I'll check it out."

Tennis camp

For the entire season, Fred was a great help to me and all those who wanted to get better at tennis. He often offered his advice and taught us the techniques he had learned in his private lessons. Any time somebody had a question about how to handle or how to hit a particular shot, he would go ask either Fred or Rafael for help. But Fred always seemed more willing to share and help than Rafael. Also, most people were closer to Fred's height and knew that they just could not do some of the things the six foot three Rafael could do.

A few of the freshmen on the team, Dylan, Nathan, Fred, Christopher, George, and me had become really close friends, and Fred invited us all to his house for a sleepover during Spring Break. George did not go, but the rest of us went to his house. Fred was the son of wealthy parents, but he and his family were generous even for people who were well off. The five of us played ping pong in his back yard, watched movies in his movie theater, and played videogames in his room as well. All the while his mom either bought takeout lunch for us or made very nice homemade meals for us. At the end of the sleepover, he bought Jamba Juice for all of us and we went to an optional but recommended tennis practice at the high school.

Fred slowly became one of my closest friends and one day in tennis practice asked me if I was interested in attending a tennis camp.

"Daniel, do you want to go to a tennis camp?" he asked.

"I want to, but I'm not sure if I can," I answered.

"Well, what else are you doing over the summer?"

"I don't know yet. Who else beside you is going?" I asked.

"Well Nathan and Dylan said that they're going. And Christopher doesn't know yet," he said.

"Okay, let me ask my parents about it and I'll get back to you maybe tomorrow or something," I said.

"Yeah, and just in case you decide to sign up, it's the Nike Tennis Camp at UC Santa Cruz. And you just go to their website and sign up for the overnight camp since we won't be coming home every single day. The date that Dylan, Nathan and I signed up for was August 2nd to August 8th and I forgot how much it costs but I think you should go," he said.

"Yeah, I'll ask my parents, it sounds good," I said.

SINCE THE TENNIS camp was in August and all the summer classes I was taking were ended by the end of July, my parents agreed for me to go to the tennis camp. The price for a week was pretty hefty and I had a feeling it wouldn't be worth it but still looked forward to it anyway.

My dad drove me down to University of California, Santa Cruz, which is located at a very nice spot near the Pacific Ocean. I was one of the last ones to get there in the group, and found out that I was rooming with Christopher. However, I noticed that originally I was supposed to room with Dylan and Nathan and Fred was supposed to room with Christopher but the spots had changed. I didn't mind rooming with Christopher but I was much better friends with Dylan and Nathan. However, I never brought it up since we were all together the entire time anyways. Plus I was sure that Christopher wouldn't be as goofy as the other two and that meant I could get more sleep at night.

We stayed in dorms that were about ten minutes walk from the tennis courts which was a little bit frustrating. The entire walk down to the courts was downhill which meant that walking back was all uphill. The food court was also directly across from the dorms. So we had to walk back and forth probably ten times a day.

The counselors at the camp were very impressed by the five of us who all came from one school. However, when Davis Cup teams were formed, I was the odd one out. Dylan and Nathan were on the same team, and Fred and Christopher were on the same team. It was a bummer for me since I didn't really know anybody else and kept to myself.

Fred was by far the best player, and was ranked #3 out of the ten players on his team. Dylan and I were both ranked #8 while Nathan and Christopher were ranked #10 on their teams. There were six teams in total and we played two matches a day. Everybody played both a doubles and a singles match. Whichever team had more total wins got the victory. I am ashamed to say that I did not win a single doubles or singles Davis Cup match.

The camp was over faster than any of us would have liked. The five of us became even closer friends and I thought that we had formed a group of friends for the rest of high school.

FRED AND I continued to be close throughout our sophomore year. But he kept on saying that he wasn't going to join the tennis team this year. People didn't believe him because he was the most tennis crazed out of everyone on the team.

Sure enough, by the time the first day of try-outs came around, he was there ready to go. He was also the most enthusiastic one. Murmurs about how weird he was started going around. I tried not to get into it, but I did find it very unusual that he would denounce the team the entire year and then come back and join. But it didn't seem to hurt our friendship. In fact, when I was losing my very first challenge match of the season to a lower ranked player, I went to him for advice. In the end I came back from a 5-1 deficit to win 7-5 and thanked him for his help. Fred himself challenged for the #1 ranking on the team, and pulled it off by beating Rafael 6-4. I was really happy for him and incredibly impressed because when he said he was going to do it, nobody believed that he could do it.

However, more things were being spread around. It had long been a pattern of his to talk badly about someone behind their back. I knew because I often went to lunch with him. If Nathan came along, he would praise Nathan and tell Nathan how well he was improving. If George tagged along he might put down Nathan and tell George how to get more consistency on his backhand.

"George, Daniel! Do you want to go to Chef's?" Fred asked.

"I'll go," I said.

"Sure, whatever," George said.

We walked about a block where I talked to George about the Spanish test we had just taken while Fred walked beside us and occasionally laughed. Soon the topic shifted, as it always does, to the tennis team.

"Hey Daniel," said Fred, "Can you tell Nathan to stop messing around so much at practice?"

"Why don't you tell him? I don't mind it ha-ha, I do the same thing along with him," I said laughing.

"No you don't mess around as much as him. He's screwing up the entire practice for everyone," Fred continued.

"What are you talking about?" said George.

"I know what you're talking about but you never had a problem with it before," I said, "What happened?"

"I don't know at first it was funny, but now Nathan's just being stupid. He sucks at tennis anyways and now he doesn't even try and only messes around in practice. It's bad for the team," Fred said.

"But why do you want me to say it?" I asked.

"Because you're his doubles partner," he said.

"Okay, but I don't think him messing around is hurting our doubles team. You think it's hurting the team and you're a teammate so you should tell him what you think," I said.

"Fine whatever," Fred said and barely said another word for the rest of lunch.

I ACTUALLY THOUGHT that Fred was going to talk to Nathan because he seemed serious about it, but he never approached Nathan during practice. A couple of days later, I went to lunch with Nathan and Fred. I thought Fred might say to Nathan what he said told me to do, but instead he acted as if he really enjoyed Nathan's goofing around.

I never told people about what he said negatively about them behind their back and was also naïve to think that he didn't do the same thing with me. But one conversation I walked in on changed everything.

"Dude, Nathan, Fred was talking hella shit about you yesterday when he came to lunch with me and Gabe," said Sean Chang, a well-respected junior and my doubles partner from last year.

"What? Are you serious? What'd he say about me?" Nathan asked.

"I don't know just stuff like, Nathan should stop always messing around in practice because he's not even that good. He just says stuff about tennis and stuff," said Robin Zhang, a junior who had just made varsity.

"Wow, all he says in front of me is how good I am," Nathan said, "Fuckin' kiss up."

"Yeah," I chimed in, "he does that all the time. I just never told you guys before. Rob, he says stuff about you too."

"So does he just talk shit about everyone behind their back? Because when we walked to Chef's today, all he was doing is telling me how good my backhand was and how to be more consistent on it. What does he say about me in when I'm not there?"

"Okay do you know how he got new rackets?" I said.

"Yeah," said Robin, Sean, and Nathan at the same time.

"So I asked him why he got new rackets when he just got new rackets last year. Like I know he's rich but it still seemed weird to me. And he told me that he didn't want to have the same racket as Christopher and Robin. He said something like 'I don't mind having the same racket as Christopher, at least Christopher is a good player. But I don't want to have the same racket as that wannabe player Gabe.' Yeah I was hella surprised when he said that," I said.

"Wow, what a dick," Sean said.

"Hella disingenuous," said Nathan.

"Okay, I'm not talking to him no more. Daniel, do you want to know what he says about you? It's not as bad as what he said about me but he just says stuff like. All Daniel does is mess around and its pissing me off. He should get kicked off the team blah blah blah," said Robin.

"Yeah, and he says the same thing about you too Nathan," Sean added.

Nathan looked at me and said, "Okay, screw his ass. I'm not going to talk to him anymore."

"Wow, why does he do that? I mean everyone talks shit about people behind their backs, I do it all the time. But I don't automatically kiss up to them when I'm in front of them. I think the combination of the two things is hella weird. But yeah, if he's going to be like this then I ain't going to talk to him anymore," I said.

"Damn, I knew he was a kiss up. That shit is obvious but I never knew he just backstabbed everyone," Nathan said.

"He roasted me pretty bad," Robin said with a laugh and we all laughed.

"So what man," I said, "Oh look he's here, let's all like turn around and not look at him."

"I can't believe this dude. After we cheer him on at all his damn matches and congratulate his ass when he beat Rafael, all he does is talk shit about us behind our backs and kiss up and tell us what we want to hear when we're around? What the fuck dude," said Nathan.

"Look away," Robin whispered as well all tried to hide our smile. As soon as he walked past us, Nathan stuck two middle fingers up right behind his head and we all burst out laughing.

IN ADDITION TO talking smack about some of us behind our backs, Fred also began to act differently around us. During tennis practice, he'd often take the handle of his racket and stick it between someone's legs or poke someone's butt with it. Often times when we walked up to him to have a conversation, he would run his hand up and down our arm and squeeze it and complement us on our muscles. Since I no longer thought highly of him and didn't value our fading friendship as much as I used to, I began to joke about how he was gay. Maybe it wasn't the nicest thing to do, but it wasn't totally out there, I certainly wasn't the only one who thought that about him.

Fred certainly wasn't unaware of his worsening reputation. He definitely sensed that many on the team did not like him as much as they used to, and changed his attitude toward us. Sometimes, he said what he said behind our backs to our faces, but made sure to say these things with a laugh as if he was joking.

It was close to the beginning of the tennis season of our sophomore year of high school, and I was playing tennis with George one Friday after school. It was one of the hottest and sunniest days of the year, and neither George nor I was having a particularly great day hitting the ball. After about an hour of frustrating tennis, Fred walked by the tennis court and started commenting on our playing.

"George, you practiced every single day and you still can't beat me right now I bet. I haven't played in probably two months," Fred said.

"Shut up! I can beat you now," George said before hitting a forehand seven feet long.

"Look at that," Fred continued, "I'll play you right now in jeans and with my backpack on and I'd still beat you. If you get four games on me during the set, I'll give you twenty bucks, but if you don't get four games, you give me five."

"Fine, play me," George said.

"Well I don't have my racket with me right now," said Fred, "Daniel, can I borrow your racket?"

"No, I'm playing right now," I said.

"Come on, it will take like twenty minutes for me to beat him," said Fred.

I saw George roll his eyes, and I said, "Sure it will. Play him next week or something."

Fred started to walk around the court since the door into the court was on the other side. He walked in the door and stood close to me while I was rallying. I didn't want to accidentally hit him with my racket on a backswing so I told him to move back.

"If I get out of your way, can I borrow your racket to play George?" he asked.

"No," I said.

Fred stormed off and we never talked again.

Chapter Three

I WAS ALSO suspended for cyberbullying Harrison Oh. Harrison was never as close a friend to me as Fred was, but we certainly didn't always hate each other. But he got on a lot of nerves when he made bold predictions about the tennis team without any proof or any chance to prove.

My freshman year was the first year that Chester High School had a men's tennis team in a while. A lot of people were excited to see a flyer for a tennis team informational meeting.

"HELLO EVERYONE, AND welcome to the tennis meeting. My name is Dorothea Gutierrez, and I am the parent coordinator of the tennis team. This is my son Rafael and this is coach James Bake. This is the first year in a while that Chester has had a men's tennis team. I'm going to let Coach Bake make any remarks he feels are necessary."

"Well, I have been a tennis coach for over 15 years but I've never coached a high school team before so this should be fun. I'm really looking forward to this season. We're going to set up some meetings before tryouts. I hear that there is also this tournament fundraiser? Do you want to talk about that Dorothea?"

"Yes, on November 17th, which is a Saturday, we're going to have a round robin tennis tournament. The fee is $10 for students and $25 for adults. Umm, there's going to be a barbeque there as well, and people have already volunteered to get food for us. So, I'm going to pass around the sign-up sheet and be sure to sign up for the tournament." Dorothea instructed.

"And also try to get more people interested in the team. I think we need at least fourteen on varsity and it would be nice to have a jayvee as well, so the more people the better." added Rafael.

"So what will the tryouts be like James?" asked Dorothea.

"I think that we're going to have a three day tryout. Probably the first day I'm going to let everyone just hit around and from that I'll be able to see basically who can play and who can't play. Then we'll have challenge matches, you know, when people just play each other and the best records make the team. So on and so forth. Should be fun. Also, the team is structured as four singles players, and six doubles players, making three doubles teams. So that would be the top ten players play the matches. The next four on varsity will be subs, so aim for the top ten."

"Well, does anyone have any questions for James or in general?" asked Dorothea.

"I'm not sure if you mentioned this, but when do tryouts start?" asked Marshall, a sophomore with curly brown hair.

Guilty Until Proven Innocent

"Uh, I would think late January or early February, because the matches start in mid February." James answered.

"What should we do to get ready for the tryouts?" asked Dylan, a freshman.

"Take lessons and just play a lot of tennis. The more you play the better you'll get. Take lessons, I'm available, there are other teachers as well but just try to hit as many balls as you can before coming to tryouts."

I didn't say anything during the meeting. But I did look around and see who was there and tried to predict what kind of spot I could get on the team.

THE NEXT TUESDAY in P.E. class, Harrison Oh, a tennis team hopeful walked up to George and I to ask about the meeting.

"Hey guys," Harrison said, "What happened at the meeting, I couldn't go yesterday."

"Why not?" I asked.

"Why won't you just tell me what happened. I don't even know why you two went. You guys aren't going to make the team." Said Harrison, somehow irritated.

"Whatever, just tell me what happened," Harrison continued.

"No, you should have went. If you think you're so raw," Said George.

"Well I heard that there's going to be a tournament. You guys going?"

"yea, I am," said George.

"Well I whoop yo ass!" yelled Harrison with a big smile. And skipped back to his assigned spot on the gym floor.

George looked at me with an arched eyebrow, "Do you really think he's as good as he says he is?"

"I don't know. He doesn't seem to be too good at other sports. But I'm not sure. We'll see in a couple weeks."

"I heard him say that him, Omar, and Rafael are going to be the only three useful players on the team."

"Yeah right," I laughed.

"Okay! Everyone start touching your toes now!" Mr. Robson hollered.

"Are you going to take some lessons?" I asked George.

"I think I'm going to take them with Dylan."

"Hmm, I might take them with Marshall or something. Wait, who are you going to take lessons from?"

"Him, James," said George.

"Alright, I guess I will too. You think we can make varsity?"

"I don't know."

"Hey! Quit talking and focus on the stretches!" Robson yelled at us.

When it was time for the sprints, Harrison lined up on the baseline next to us and began asking us questions about tennis.

"What racket do you guys use?" he asked.

"I have a Dunlop one. It's green," Said George.

"Dunlop hella weak dude! You think you can play well with those rackets? I have a Wilson N-code. $180 dollar racket. Get one of those and maybe you can play tennis," smirked Harrison.

"The tools are only as good as the workman," I replied.

"Wow really? Shut up, just because you suck at tennis. Don't hate bro, don't hate. Just wait until that tournament. I'll whoop yo ass. Hey Emre, who do you think is better at tennis. Me or Daniel?"

"I haven't seen either of you play. So I can't decide," answered Emre.

"Exactly Harrison, stop talking about it. It's getting annoying," I said.

"See me at the tournament!" Harrison yelled, and ran off again.

BEFORE PE CLASS with Harrison and all the tennis stuff went on, I had only encountered Harrison a couple of times. He seemed to be a popular guy since many people talked about him, but nobody ever said anything good about him.

Harrison's birthday was in September, he was very young for our grade and teenage boys have the habit of giving each other birthday punches. My toughest year was thirteen, because the middle school I went to announced everybody's birthday on the public address at the start of each school day. I came home with a lot of bruises on my arms. But I didn't bare any animosity toward people, nor did I have any interest in punching anyone on their birthday.

It was now freshman year and Harrison had just turned fourteen. We were in the same advisory class along with some other people who didn't think so highly of him. Nobody did much in advisory so word got around that it was Harrison's birthday. Patrick, who was sitting next to me, called Harrison over. Harrison strutted over and said, "What's up Patrick?"

Patrick stood up and said to Harrison, "Heard it's your birthday man!"

Harrison's face turned a little bit pale as he answered, "Yeah it is ha-ha. I'm fourteen now!"

Patrick raised up a fist and faked a punch to Harrison's arm but before Patrick even pulled back, Harrison had turned around and leapt. He knocked over a stand but quickly picked it up. Since Harrison was making so much noise, the entire class had looked over at him and laughing. He turned around at Patrick and we saw how red his face had gotten, he yelled, "Wow Patrick, really? Grow up already!"

Patrick then charged at Harrison and grabbed his two arms thus sort of leaving him helpless as he stood there.

"Daniel!" Patrick yelled between laughs, "Get your punches in!"

I backed away a little bit and said, "Nah I don't like to do birthday punches."

Patrick smiled and shook his head, "Come on man, I got him for you!"

Patrick then let Harrison go who yelled at Patrick, "Look Patrick, Daniel is actually mature he doesn't give birthday punches!" He then stormed off to his seat, sat down and read a book.

"You know you wanted to sock him," Patrick said after Harrison was out of hearing distance.

"Ha-ha maybe. This was too cheap though and I could only get him on the arm. If we actually did punch him he'd probably get us in trouble." I said.

"Hell yeah he would, did you see how scared his punk ass got?" Patrick said as he laughed.

"Yeah, I bet if it was somebody else's birthday and they didn't care about birthday punches he would probably be first in line to get his punches in," I said.

"Probably," said Patrick.

A MONTH LATER, it was George's birthday. George was one of the younger people in our grade as well and was turning fourteen in October. One day, Patrick, Dylan, George, and I were spending break outside of the computer lab on the first floor. Dylan, Patrick, and I had given George baby birthday punches, pretty much just touching him on the shoulder fourteen times with our fists, George didn't even care and just stood there as we continued a conversation. At this time, Harrison walked up and bust into the little chat circle we had formed.

"Yo! Is it George's birthday?" he asked,

"No it's not," George said.

"Then why were they all punching you?" Harrison asked.

"None of your business," George said.

"It is your birthday don't lie," said Harrison, "Here Daniel hold this." Harrison tried to hand me his books but I let them drop to the ground.

"Wow Daniel, thanks," said Harrison as he raised up his fists and prepared to give George his birthday punches.

"What the fuck are you doing?" George said, "Get out of here."

"Wow, quit being such a baby, it's just some birthday punches."

Patrick and I looked at each other and began laughing uncontrollably. Harrison had a short memory it seems.

In the end, Harrison didn't give George very hard punches, but he put some weight into them and George had to flex his arm to brace for them.

Later on, Patrick and I took turns telling George and Dylan what had happened with Harrison on his birthday.

I WOKE UP that Saturday morning early and excited about the upcoming tennis tournament. I picked a Chicago White Sox 2005 World Series Championship shirt and gray Adidas shorts. When I arrived, some of the parents had already arrived. Marshall Williams' parents were setting up two small grills and lined up a couple coolers of soft drinks and waters. Marshall had his racket in his hand, and looked ready to go.

"Hi Daniel, thanks for coming," Mrs. Graham said.

"Hi Mrs. Graham."

"Do you want to go warm up with Marshall? I think people are going to start pouring in pretty soon."

"Sure," I said, and walked toward Marshall.

I hit with Marshall for about twenty minutes before some other players came and joined on our court. Everyone was hitting quietly and calmly before Harrison came.

"Hey what's up everyone," Harrison said as he walked onto the middle of our court. So far it had been four people. Two on each side, hitting ground strokes to one another. Harrison walked onto the court and began volleying the balls that he could reach.

"Wow," I muttered under my breath.

"Yeah, there are two open courts over there. Why does he come here and mess our nice rally session up?" Omar said.

"You want to go on those other courts?" I asked.

"Yeah, let's go."

"Let's get all the other people too, and leave Harrison on this court by himself."

"Nah, let's just go hit by ourselves," Omar laughed.

When twenty or so people had assembled on the courts to hit, Dorothea called everyone in to give instructions about how the tournament would take place.

"So, it's going to be all doubles. I think we have the entire round robin sorted out," she started.

"Do we get to pick our own doubles partners?" Harrison interrupted.

"No, we're all going to alternate partners to make sure that it's as fair a competition as we can make it. Anyways, we're going to play four game matches. And after each match come to this table where we have everyone's name written and tell us how many out of those four games you won. So pretend you tied against the other team two-two, so come tell us two, and we'll record that next to your name. At the end of the tournament, the person with the most total games will win a prize. Bob, you want to show everyone the prizes for a little extra motivation?"

"Well, we have two first prizes. They are these UC Berkeley tennis shirts. We have two of these. Second prize is a $30 gift card to Plaza Tennis, which is on Tamarac. Very friendly people operating that store. And the third prize is a Chester Tennis water bottle," said Mr. Graham.

"So, without further ado, let's begin this tournament."

I was assigned to play two adults on a court. My partner was a girl who I had never met before, but just from the warm up hitting that we did before the match began, I could tell that she was a serious tennis player, and that the other team didn't really stand a chance since they were just casual players who had never had formal training.

After winning the mini-match 4-0, I recorded my score at the table. At that time, Harrison walked over me and asked to see my racket. I handed it to him and he examined it up close, far away, and up close again.

"Hmm, it's head heavy."

"What does that mean?" I asked.

"It means it sucks. Well it doesn't suck, but it's a beginner's racket."

"Well, I'm a beginner. So I guess this racket fits me perfectly. When I'm not a beginner anymore I'll get a better racket." I said rather humbly.

"Actually, I watched you a little bit. You don't suck as much as I thought you did."

"Thanks," I said, and walked over to Dylan, who had just arrived, before Harrison could start another lecture on tennis.

After everyone had played a few matches, Mr. Graham called everyone in for lunch. It was a pretty classic picnic with hot dogs, burgers, potato salad, chips, and sodas. I had gotten so into the tennis that I did not eat much before I was playing again.

I just realized that the entire time the tournament had been going on, I did not look at the scoreboard. When I did, I found out that I was in first place and coincidentally, my next match was against Harrison.

His team won the toss, and he decided to serve first.

Immediately, it seemed to me that he did not play like an elite level tennis player. His motions weren't very smooth or graceful or even powerful. I always knew he wasn't a particularly good athlete by seeing him struggle at many sports in physical education class, but I figured he would be well practiced enough in tennis to look good.

Another thing I noticed was how self conscious he was when he played. Once, he whiffed a forehand and began to look around. George and Dylan, who were leaning against the fence watching, started to giggle a little bit at Harrison's embarrassing miss.

"Wow guys, I'm trying to play a match. It's called not being warmed up yet," Harrison shot at Dylan and George.

The match ended with the score tied at 2-2. My partner and I went up to shake hands with Harrison and his partner. At the time, all he said was good match but when his partner wasn't around he said to me.

"You have to admit. If I had a better partner, we would have won that match probably 3-1."

"Yeah, probably," I said.

"You should work on your backhand," he continued.

"I know."

"I mean, your forehand is okay but you made a lot of errors with your backhand," he said, "If you fixed your backhand maybe you could make the team. I think you should switch a grip, that might be the problem."

I didn't respond.

"Good luck during tryouts. I told you I was gonna beat you," said Harrison.

"You didn't beat me. We tied," I said.

"Well, your partner was better than my partner. But I played better than you did. So basically I beat you."

"Wow, sure."

"Don't be mad. Fix your crap-ass backhand."

He walked off and left me sitting there myself. George walked up to me and said, "Dude, he's not that good."

"Not as good as he said he was," I said, "Did you see Fred?"

"Yeah, he's been playing for five years."

"He's really good. He might be better than Omar."

"Harrison said he can beat Fred," George said.

"Ha-ha, sure. I'm gonna check to see if I can play another match."

By the end of the tournament, half the people who were trying out for the team with the exception of Rafael, Omar, and Fred had gotten a five minute tennis lesson from Harrison. He started to give me one when I ignored him. It turned out that he won six games total from four matches he played. I tied with Dylan for first place. Neither of us was a very good player yet, but we had gotten lucky by getting good doubles partners and over-achieving a little.

There were two University of California, Berkeley tennis shirts for the two of us. He won the rock-paper-scissors between us and got a first pick between the two shirts. I appreciated the shirt, but also learned where I stood compared to others that looked like they were going to try out for the team. I didn't have any expectations for myself yet but just looked forward to making it onto the team. I now believed that I had a chance to make the team.

"ALRIGHT GUYS, WELCOME to tryouts. I'm uh, excited to see that so many people showed up. So, let me introduce myself. I'm James Bake. I work for the city of Chester as a tennis coach. You may have seen me on these courts or at courts at Ocean View coaching, mostly young kids. I know a few of you guys who have taken lessons from me. How about for now, let's just go around and each say your name and what year you're in."

Rafael, the leader among the group, started and everybody said their name and year.

"Good. Now, let's not waste any time. How about everyone does ten laps around these two courts right here. Run hard guys, this is your warm up."

After everybody jogged their ten laps, James mixed up into groups to volley. I was in a group with Rafael, Oscar, and Josh. There was one ball for the four of us on that court, and we had to keep the ball in play. The first person to mess up five times had to do twenty pushups.

It was clear right away that Oscar was a much better player than the rest of us. While Josh and I could volley all the balls hit our way over the net, Oscar was doing different spins and had much better form and technique.

While we did these exercises, James walked around all four courts checking up on how everyone was doing. He would occasionally make a remark about technique.

"Josh, for that high backhand volley, you want to keep your wrist firm. Don't bend that wrist no matter what. Move your elbows and shoulders but keep that wrist firm. I know you kids all watch Federer do those fancy backhand smashes and he snaps his wrist. But, you know, he's a freak, we can't do what he does. So to make sure that your volleys are clean, keep your wrist tight and firm."

After volleying for about 20 minutes, we moved on to one-on-one rallies. Teams of five or six were formed, and one person from each team would play a point. If the person won a point, he would stay on, but if he lost, he would go to the back and wait his turn. I was on opposite teams with Harrison, and he could not keep up with players like Oscar and Josh who were on my team. When Josh was at the back of the line behind me, I talked to him about Harrison.

"Dude, why does Harrison suck? Do you remember when he said that he, Omar, Oscar, and Rafael would be the only four useful players on the team and that everyone else sucked?"

"Don't worry about it Daniel, you're better than him. All he does is talk big."

"I guess, but you're going to have to teach me that forehand of yours someday."

"You think it's good?"

"It's hella good, especially on a weak shot. It's game over for the other guy."

"Ha-ha, thanks, but my backhand and serve aren't that good yet. I got to work on those before we play matches." Josh said.

"Yup," I replied, and walked up to play a point.

After about an hour of tryouts, James seemed to know who he thought were good players and who he thought were the more intermediate players, as he called them.

"So guys, I'm going to split you guys up. These two lower courts are going to be for the more advanced players, and the upper courts will be for the beginning players. I'm judging you guys right now on a very limited sample so please don't get angry if you think you have been placed on the wrong courts. Just show me that I'm wrong by playing well and we'll move you accordingly."

Thankfully, I was placed on a lower court with the more advanced group. Each court had a bucket of tennis balls, and we lined up to do some serving.

The lessons from James had helped a lot. I now had better technique on all of my shots and especially my serve which proved to be among the faster ones.

"I'm liking the speed on that serve Daniel. See if you can get some spin and still keep that speed." James said.

I was about to try what he had just suggested before a couple of loud pops rang from the other lower court. It was Rafael's serve. One of his serves had hit the top of the net cord, causing two back-to-back loud pops. One when he hit the ball and one when it snapped on the cord.

For a couple of seconds, all serving on our court stopped as every watched Rafael serve another time. We were probably all hoping for another flat, hard serve, but this time Rafael brushed the ball, causing it to bounce about six feet high when it bounced on the other side.

"That's a kick serve guys. When you guys can all serve like Rafael, we'll have a really strong team. Those are just two monster serves." James said, and walked over to the court Rafael was on.

"Oh my god," George said, "It's not fair, he's hella tall."

"I know!" Josh yelled, "It's impossible for me to serve that fast, he's a foot taller than me! What the hell!"

"Well, there's nothing we can do about it. Let's keep serving, come on," Morgan said, offering his senior words of advice.

For about fifteen minutes, we all served, and then got in line to watch Rafael serve. At that point, we knew that we had a bona fide number one singles player, but we wondered if any of the rest of us would be good enough to hold up the rest of the team.

When the first day of tryouts was over, James Bake called everyone onto a court. It was dark already, and the lights beamed onto the court.

"Alrighty guys, how was it?"

"Good" was the most common answer.

"So tomorrow," James continued, "you can expect about the same thing. Some mini tennis and volleys for warm-up. Then some games of single rallies. Some serving, some drills. Except tomorrow, this court will be for the four players who have shown that they are head and shoulders above the rest. Well, not head and shoulders, but who have shown the most capability today. That's Fred, Omar, Rafael, and Oscar. So tomorrow, you guys will be on that court alone with some drills that I'll tell you to do, and the rest of you will be on the rest of these three courts fighting for spots. Also, tomorrow Sue will be here. Sue Ford is the women's tennis coach here at Chester high and has been kind enough to volunteer to coach the JV for us. So you know, only fourteen people make varsity. But, *everybody* else will be allowed to participate on JV, so keep coming out and hitting. You are all welcome to come and hit tennis balls as long as you guys don't mess around."

"How can we get better really fast?" Carlos asked.

"Hit. And hold your racket more. Get a feel for that grip, whatever grip you use on your forehand, your serve, your backhand. You know. In the car don't just leave your racket in your bag, take it out and hold it. Also, you just got to get out here or onto any courts and just hit balls. That's the only way to get better. And you know, it's going to take time. Tennis is a sport just like any other sport. I sometimes hear people who talk like they're going to get good at tennis in a month and start playing regularly. That doesn't happen. You can't get good at basketball, soccer, or football in a month and you can't get good at tennis in a month. You can make a lot of progress. And that's all we're asking here. Our first match is a little less than one month away. So, I'd just advise you all to hit tennis balls whenever you can. I know some of you have a lot of homework, tests to study for, but when you have time hit balls. It will help everyone. Any more questions?"

"Same time tomorrow?" Harrison asked.

"Same time, same place. And bring an attitude of wanting to get better at tennis, not I want a spot on the team. Everybody makes the JV. And you guys have Sue who will work with you guys. So if there are no more questions, you all are excused. If you want to stay longer, I'll leave a few balls here and you can hit. Just bring them back tomorrow. Alright, thanks guys." James said and clapped his hands.

Most people got their rackets to pack up a leave, as some parents were already waiting outside the courts for their kids. I called my dad to come pick me up.

While I was waiting, I walked over to George and Dylan who were still hitting.

"So," I said as I approached George, "What did we learn today?"

"That freshmen can't make varsity," said George a little bit dejectedly.

"Wait what?" I said in disbelief.

"Yeah didn't you hear? Omar said that freshmen can't make varsity and that seniors make it for sure."

"Well Sparks and Morgan would probably have made it anyways."

"They aren't that good. But they probably would make it." George said.

"Well, what else did we learn today?"

"Harrison sucks!"

"Yup, he really does. Like at that tennis tournament in November, he could still keep up with us, now he's just totally on another level."

"What are you talking about?" George asked, "He sucked at that tournament in November too. I knew he was just talking smack the whole damn time."

"Only four useful players. Him, Omar, Oscar, and Rafael."

"Yeah right. Even if he wasn't a freshmen, he still wouldn't make varsity."

"He wouldn't make varsity if he was a senior." I said.

"Ha-ha yup."

"That kind of sucks. So we'll be on JV for a year. We're definitely going to make var next year though."

"We better. Look, we should make it this year too."

"Exactly, I honestly don't think there are 14 players better than us. Like the team will be older but it's not going to be as good if there are none of the freshmen on it because we're the better players."

"Hey! Are you guys talking about me over there?" Dylan asked.

"No! Shut the hell up! We're talking about James Bakes bullshit policies." George yelled.

"Ha-ha, calm down. I bet we'll make var."

"Omar already told us we can't make it."

"What about Fred. He already got put on that good court."

"Oh yeah huh? I bet he gets an exception because he's way better."

"Well I'll see you later, my dad's here." I said.

"See ya," George said.

"Bye!" Dylan yelled.

FESHMAN YEAR PE class was always interesting. For the girls, it was a challenge to not get too sweaty and nasty. For the boys it was a chance to show off what athletic ability they had or hide their lack of it. It seemed that for most people, they knew if they were or were not athletic. Harrison was not one of these people.

The first time I noticed that he wasn't as athletic as he looked was during warm ups one day. We always ended warm-ups by doing ten sprints down and back on the basketball court. A lot of guys tried to race each other during this time and Harrison decided to participate in that day's race. One of the people that was racing that day was Daryl Jones, a track athlete who participated in the 100 meters, 200 meters, and long jump. Harrison wanted to race him.

For the first couple of races, Daryl was not going very hard, just keeping up with everyone else. However, Harrison, perhaps not realizing that Daryl was giving less than full effort, began talking to Daryl.

"Yo is that how fast all the track stars at our school are? No wonder we never win a track meet!" Harrison looked around for some laughing approval but none came.

"So far I've been about tied with you Daryl, but I'm gonna beat you on these next seven!" Harrison shouted at Daryl.

Daryl looked at his friend Edward next to him and simply smiled. He then walked to where Harrison was standing and got in a stance next to Harrison.

"Let's go," whispered Daryl.

Mr. Robson blew the whistle and they took off. Daryl took small compact steps and pumped his arms in rhythm with his legs. Harrison took long gaping steps that left his arms flinging about. Weirdly, Harrison kept up with Daryl for about twenty feet, but Daryl's strides began to get longer and faster and Harrison had no chance. On the way back down the court, Daryl jogged the last half. Harrison had already given up on the race anyways.

"Next one," Harrison huffed loudly.

"Sure," said Daryl.

On the next race, Daryl decided to start his race a little while after Harrison started his. When Mr. Robson blew the whistle, Daryl waited for Harrison to reach the free throw line and then burst from the line, caught, and passed Harrison. Harrison, although impressed, seemed to not realize how badly he was being beaten. He was completely out of breath and said, "Last one up next, I'm a bit out of shape."

"Okay, last one," said Daryl.

During the resting period, Harrison could barely stand up straight. Daryl was breathing heavily as well but looked to be merely warmed up as opposed to tired. For the last race, Daryl must have had something special planned. Winning the race was not an issue whatsoever, it was about how many style points he received while winning.

Daryl took off on the whistle this time and ran as hard as he could. When he got to the opposite side of the court, he did not bother to turn around. He simply ran backwards for essentially the second half of the race. Harrison, to be fair, had been tired out from the previous races and probably wasn't going his fastest, but after that day he rarely participated in races between people at the end of warm ups.

I ARRIVE AT tryouts the next day with the goal to give maximum effort on everything the coach said in order to be a freshmen player on the varsity tennis team. In middle school, I had heard high school kids talking about how impressive a sophomore on a varsity sports team was, and how incredible the freshmen must be if he or she made var. I knew that I had a chance and that if I worked harder than the other freshmen that were around my level, that I would make it. I didn't even care if I got playing time or not, I just wanted to make the team.

We started off with the same run, ten laps around the two lower courts. I ran harder and found myself running with Dylan, who also felt like running harder than we had the previous day. After the run, I was a little tired and was worried about my endurance for the rest of the day's tryouts.

Right away, the four top players were put on a separate court where they played points against each other. Six players, include me, were put on the other lower court. I saw this as a good sign because all of the players that weren't as good were all on the higher courts. This included George and he was a little bit upset.

When the water break finally arrived, people huddled around to chat a little bit. George walked up to me and began to talk while shaking his head.

"I can't believe this. Dylan is on the good court and I'm stuck with those guys," he fumed.

"Don't worry. At least you're with the best player on the team Harrison Oh. That should be an honor for you," I said.

"Ha-ha, dude he sucks."

"Where is he? I want to rub it in his face. Giving me crap all the time about sucking at tennis and him being so damn great. Now where he at? He's on the weak court and he doesn't even deserve to be on any court."

"I'm on that court too. So I can't say anything."

"Yeah but you'll be on the good court soon. He won't be. Let's go talk to him."

"You can, I'll just watch."

I saw Harrison talking to Sean and Nathan. At first I didn't talk to him and just listened to what Harrison was saying.

"It's so BS. All he's doing is putting the people on who take lessons with him on the good courts because they paid him."

"What up almighty Harrison?" I chimed in.

"Shut up Daniel. You know you're only on that court because you took lessons from him right."

"Mhm, which is why Marshall and George aren't on that court right."

"No, they just suck. I admit, you're pretty good, but not that good."

"You do realize that the four top players, Fred, Omar, Rafael, and Oscar don't take lessons from him so you know. Your argument makes no sense."

"Omar and Rafael spend hella time kissing up to him. Oscar is a beast and Fred is a beast."

"Wow," said George.

"Shut up George! You took lessons with him and you're still on the crap courts. That means you suck hella much!" Harrison said.

"Play me then damn! All you've done is talk trash."

"Yeah, shut up Harrison. You said that you were a top four player. And the top four don't take lessons from James so it shouldn't affect you. But you're not even in the top ten. What happened?" taunted Nathan.

"I'm a little out of practice. You do admit I should be on the top ten right?"

"No." said Sean.

"My ass," said George.

"Ha-ha hell no." I said.

"Screw you guys. When challenge matches come, I'll beat you guys and see if you guys keep talking trash to me."

"I can't believe that guy," I said, "He spent like four months telling us how much we suck and how good he is. And he comes here and can't play at all and still gives some stupid ass excuses."

"Dude don't worry about him," Sean said.

"And now look at him trying to talk to Oscar. Oscar doesn't want to talk to that fool," I said.

"Chill out. Look James is back, let's go back to our good court Daniel," said Sean, "Kidding guys, I'm just kidding."

After another pretty tiring day, James Bake called everyone in again to explain what would be happening. Harrison sat right in front of me.

"So guys, tomorrow is Wednesday right? Okay, we're going to start challenge matches. You guys can challenge whoever you want as long as the person you challenge agrees to play you. Um, it's on a first come first serve basis. Three courts will be for challenge matches, and the fourth court will be for everyone to just hit on," said the coach.

"Okay, finally something I can prove myself at," Harrison said, "Wait coach, when do we sign up for challenges?"

"Tomorrow at tryouts I'll have a little notepad where you the two of you who have agreed to play a challenge match come up and tell me so. And I'll put you down. So think about who is on a similar level with you and play them. That's how you are going to move up the ladder. Also I'll have a ladder tomorrow just based on what I've seen so far. And that should give you an idea of where you stand. It won't be perfect but it's what I think."

TWENTY-ONE HOURS later, I found out that I had made varsity.

Chapter Four

ON THE SURFACE Harrison looked like a good athlete. He was already about six feet tall and was built like a good soccer player, thick legs and a skinny, lean upper body. However, he was not very coordinated and thus struggled at many sports. One of the most obvious and awkward events was during basketball.

I had occasionally played basketball with Harrison before and knew that he, at the very least, wasn't all-world. We were playing three on three, and on the last day of the unit, we were allowed to pick our own teams and play whoever we wanted. This made me very happy because previously I had been assigned a team with two girls who hated basketball. But after I had formed a team with George and a six foot six guy Jason, Harrison came up with his team of two other five-two Asian girls and challenged us. We didn't want to play him but there wasn't really another team for us to play.

"We got ball first because I have two girls on my team," Harrison said as he checked George the ball.

"Okay, sure," said Jason who was on the varsity basketball team.

The two girls on his team quickly stood together on the left side of the lane, about eighteen feet from the basket. One had her arms crossed and the other clasped her hands together. This was going to be such a fun game. Harrison began busting crossovers that got him nowhere and jacked up a couple three pointers that hit nothing after it left his hand but the hardwood floor.

As for our team, all we did was passing Jason the ball who either hit a jump shot or drove to the basket and shot over Harrison with ease. Once however, Jason missed and the ball bounced toward the girls. They quickly handed the ball to Harrison who immediately shot a three and made it. George and I had been talking a little trash to him about all the shots he was missing so Harrison held up both his hands as if he was winning and said, "How do you like that sucka? Have a taste of that!"

During this time, George and I had both made various shots with little fanfare. Even the girls on his team snickered a little bit at Harrison's boastfulness.

Jason seemed to take special offense at this act and whispered to me and George, "Watch this."

"Daniel, go check the ball up top and pass it to me," Jason said.

I checked the ball to one of the girls and bounce passed it to Jason in the post. Jason dribbled hard into Harrison and forced Harrison to take a few steps backwards. Harrison regained his position and Jason once again knocked into Harrison, this time knocking him over. Now right under the basket, Jason jumped up and dunked the ball. He then walked away, pretending to brush dirt off his shoulders, alluding to the famous Jay-Z song.

AND SO MY relationship with Harrison continued. We rarely talked. On the rare days that we did, the outcome was unpredictable. Sometimes we'd share a friendly but half-hearted laugh, sometimes we'd come out disgusted at each other.

Pretty soon, we just began to ignore each other in person. However, we'd still sometimes get into little arguments here and there on Facebook. Being a social networking site where two people like me and Harrison could hurl insults at each other while miles away, things were said or typed rather that maybe we wouldn't have said in person.

Because of our not so nice relationship, Harrison and I had "defriended" each other on Facebook. He could not track what I was doing, and I could not track what he was doing. But we had mutual friends, and that's where our latest and greatest conflict began.

One day, Sean showed me Harrison's profile picture. It was a picture that Harrison took of himself. He was shirtless.

The comments on the picture were all telling him to put a shirt on or start working out. He wasn't fat, he was in decent shape. But very few people, even the muscular basketball and soccer players, set their profile pictures as semi nude pictures of themselves. The profile picture was how the whole world would see you. I saw the profile picture as the person wrapped up in one picture.

Harrison's picture was pretty narcissistic.

The next day, a lot of people began to talk about Harrison's latest picture.

One guy, who I didn't know too well, Joel Yamada, was particularly fond of making jokes about it.

"Hey guys did you all see Harrison's profile picture?" he said during English class.

"Yeah man, the guy is mad buff."

"No not just that one. Like all the previous ones. I looked at them all. Fuckin' K-pop superstar right there," Joel said.

The room wobbled with laughter.

JOEL ALSO LIKED to make fun of a guy named Karl Donald. Karl was a year older than me and Joel. When Karl walked down the hall, everyone noticed. He had the biggest watch, the thickets chains around his neck and the lowest sagging pants in the school. He probably also had the most booming voice of anyone in the school. Maybe he didn't know how to whisper, but the general perception was that he just wanted to be heard.

One day at lunch, Karl was playing basketball. Karl was probably a better basketball player than 99% of the boys at our school, but was not very good compared to the people on the basketball team. He was fast and athletic, could dribble well, but always could not finish the easy layups that he worked so hard to create for himself. Karl was also a below average shooter but liked to launch three pointers that not many people would dare attempt. As a starting guard on the school's varsity team Joel looked down on Karl and liked to make fun of Karl's game.

On this particular day, more than half the basketball team stopped to watch the game that was taking place on the outdoor courts on the school campus. Karl was arguably the best player on the court, and took most of the shots for his team.

He made a nice spin move, maybe traveled a bit, but created an easy open layup for himself. He blew it. The entire group of people on the team, including some others who weren't on the team, turned away to laugh. But Joel yelled out some sarcastic words of encouragement to Karl.

"Hey brah, don't worry about it. That was a sick move you made. Don't worry you'll make it next time. Go dumb on these fools Karl. YEE! Nobody got swag like you!" Joel yelled.

"Yeah I know man. I can't make a fuckin' layup to save my fuckin' life. I always got them open ass looks and miss so bad. Don't worry though. I got it next time check me out," Karl replied.

When Karl turned around to continue the game, Joel rolled his eyes and laughed along with the rest of the basketball team.

MONTHS EARLIER, Joel had made a sarcastic fan page for Karl Donald. Behind Karl's back, Joel and his friends all pointed out how pathetic they saw Karl to be. The group was called, *Karl Donald is my idol*. The description included reasons why Karl Donald was their hero. The picture had a picture of Karl holding up a bunch of twenty dollar bills laying back in a flashy hoody. The group had over 200 members and had a wall full of "admiring" comments toward Karl.

In the middle of Freshman year, my friend Marshall had made a fanpage named Daniel Liu. I was still naïve at the time and since Marshall and I had many classes together and constantly poked fun at each other, I did not mind the fan page. Mutual friends of ours would join the fan page but no comments were made. There were no hard feelings either.

I saw this and got an idea. I made a fan page for Harrison Oh. Facebook makes it very easy to make a fan page for someone. It took about twenty minutes out of my homework time, and I had made a fan club for Harrison. On it, I posted pictures that were mostly posted by Harrison himself onto Facebook. Under each photo, I added a "flattering" comment describing the photo of Harrison. All of the comments were saying positive things for Harrison, but the sarcastic undertone was unmistakable.

People began to join the club in bunches.

HE DID NOT respond as I thought he would, and we pretty much kept ignoring each other which was fine by me. We didn't talk for maybe two months until a mistake on his part led to a bad conversation between us.

It was after school. A bunch of people were right outside the school talking with each other before our parents came to pick us up. Harrison's house was only a few blocks away from school but he decided to stay a bit to talk to some people as well.

I was chatting with my friends Nathan and Emre while Harrison was talking to Tim. They were only a few feet away from us.

Harrison suddenly said, "All right, I'm going to get going."

After he walked a few steps, Nathan yelled out, "Yes! He's gone!"

Everybody around started to chuckle a little bit and Harrison walked right up to me.

"What did you say Daniel?" he said.

"I didn't say anything," I said, wondering what he meant.

"When I turned around, what did you say? Why don't you say it to my face?" he said.

"Harrison, are you stupid, Daniel didn't say anything," Emre said.

"Shut up Emre stay out of this," Harrison said.

"I don't even know what you're talking about Harrison," I said.

"I love how you always talk so much shit when people aren't around, but run away whenever the person actually confronts you," Harrison said.

I really could not believe that he confused my voice with Nathan's voice. Nathan had a much higher voice than me, and sounded nothing like me. I was getting a little angry myself, so I said, "I love how you always talk about how good you are at tennis but whiff whenever it's time to time to actually hit the ball."

"Okay whatever, I suck at tennis, I don't care," he said.

"Okay," I said.

"Yeah, someday when teachers aren't around. I'd like to see you talk shit then," he said and walked away.

Nathan waited until he was out of hearing distance this time and said, "What the hell was that dude?"

"Yeah," said Emre, "You two don't soundalike at all. He is so stupid."

"Ha-ha-ha," Tim laughed.

"Whatever, my dad's here. I'll talk to you guys later."

IT WAS LATE February or maybe it was early March. However, it was right after the Olympics, and I had just been mesmerized by the charm of gold medal winning figure skater Kim Yu Na, as were many people in my school. As a joke, I decided to create a fake account of Kim Yu Na, and listed her as my girlfriend. Many others went along with the joke and began to refer to me as Kim Yu Na's boyfriend. Some did it with a laugh, but my friend Robin Zhang did it religiously.

I saw him one day at a mall, where my family and I were about to eat dinner in a restaurant. As he walked by me, he called me "Kim Yu Na's Boyfriend". I laughed and he smiled, and we went our separate ways after that.

But later on Facebook, he made a joke on by saying on his status that he was jealous that "Daniel is dating Kim Yu Na". He used the new feature of Facebook that allowed him to tag both accounts in his status, sending a notification to me. Harrison Oh could apparently see the status as well, and made a comment calling me desperate and a "loser".

I was still pretty upset about what Harrison did to me that one day after school, so I did responded back. I made fun of the girls that he had dated in the past and dumped him. He threatened to "beat my ass" if I didn't stop. The conversation between us got ugly until I finally said something that angered him so much that he challenged me to a fight after math class which we had together.

A while after the argument between us stopped, Robin sent me a message telling me that Harrison had screenshotted the conversation and was ready to send it to school authorities to report me.

Initially, I thought this was an incredibly dumb move on his part. First of all, it was on Facebook and it was Sunday night. I did not believe that the school could punish me for what I did on Sunday night in my room. Second of all, he had started the ugly conversation by calling me a loser. He had also threatened to beat me up during school, so I wasn't too worried about it. However,

I took a screenshot of the conversation as well before he could maybe delete the some of his comments and frame me. If this was going to happen the evidence had to be complete. I believed he had no case against me.

At school the next day, I was anxious about being called down to the office. But nothing happened. Nothing happened for a week, so I relaxed and thought that the thing was over with. But apparently I was wrong.

SO I'VE TOLD you about Harrison and Fred. However, I'm not sure if it was enough to convey the terrible relationship we had. Maybe it was just the stupidity of high schoolers and not a big deal. But egos got in the way and it was pretty heated. Looking back, maybe it shouldn't have been.

Chapter Five

I'VE ALREADY DESCRIBED James Bake to you. And to this day I maintain that he is a very nice and easygoing guy. He was incredibly human which is a good thing, most of the time. He was incredibly nice and favorable to some and unreasonable to others.

Before the start of tennis season during my freshman year, I took lessons from James Bake with a sophomore named Marshall. The lessons were really fun, and I improved dramatically.

James was also an accomplished player from his high school and college days and taught me the traditional tennis fundamentals I wanted to learn. He also liked my potential, and said that besides being a little bit out of shape that I had good athleticism and coordination.

After five lessons with John, I had improved dramatically. James knew what he was talking about and I respected and listened to what he told me to do because I believed he knew my game better than I did and was only trying to help me improve.

I would not have had a shot at all to make the varsity team if it wasn't for James. Marshall, my tennis buddy, fell slightly short but was one of the top junior varsity players.

Freshman year on the tennis team was incredibly fun. We had a great mix of seniors, juniors, sophomores and freshmen on the team. I was happy just to be on the team and didn't' expect to be playing singles or doubles one. I was winning most of my matches playing as the second or third doubles team. I probably could have challenged a few people ranked higher than me to gain a better ranking, but did not feel compelled to. As I said, I was just incredibly happy to be there.

WHEN THE SEASON ended, the entire team had a great chemistry. The end of the year barbeque drew most of the members from both the varsity and junior varsity team. That summer, I attended tennis camp with a few friends and thought that tennis was going to be one of my main activities outside of school.

When the season started the next year, I was looking to be one of the top doubles players. I enjoyed playing doubles the year before and wanted to get better at it. Meanwhile, there was a duel for the fourth and final singles spot. At first, it seemed that George had claimed it, but after losing challenge match after challenge match, George lost it to Josh.

I picked Nathan as a doubles partner while Dylan and George teamed up. Since Dylan and George were ranked higher on the depth chart than Nathan and me they were put as the number one doubles team. I understood at the time, but made it a goal to be the number one doubles player by the middle of the season at the latest.

After the first match, Nathan and I challenged George and Dylan to a doubles match. The coach granted it. He probably had a sense that he had two really good doubles teams that were pretty even and both gave him pretty equal chances to win matches.

We started off the match quickly down 0-3. But then on my serve, George missed a couple of easy forehands which drew the ire of Dylan. They began to argue with each other. At that point, both Nathan and I knew that we had a great chance to make a quick comeback and get back into the match.

Sure enough, we tied it up at 3-3. They kept bickering at each other, but began to play better. Nathan missed a couple of first serves, and got his second serve blasted for a winner by George a couple times and we were broken again. After Dylan held serve, we found ourselves trying to dig out of a 5-3 hole.

I held serve to make it 5-4 making sure to serve to both of their backhands even if it mean taking significant speed off, but we still needed a break to stay alive. George's serve had been a little bit iffy before so we took the opportunity. It was surprisingly easy to break his serve. At that point, we had all the momentum.

Again, their return game got them back into the match. After three serves it was 0-40 for us and we were forced to fight off three break points. Nathan came up with a few big serves and a terrible forehand from Dylan and we were back to deuce.

We eventually won 7-5. It was one of the more interesting matches I had ever played. In high school tennis, momentums don't shift very often. Most victories are pretty straightforward but I was really proud of both me and Nathan for fighting back and coming up with the win. We now had all the confidence that we were the best doubles team and thought that we would be playing number one doubles in the upcoming match.

STRANGELY, THAT WASN'T the case. Against St. Mary's, our biggest challenge the whole year, Nathan and I were still placed as the number two doubles team. We won our match easily against St. Mary's and approached the coach about his decision.

"What's up guys? Nice win," James said as he gave both Nathan and me a fist bump.

"Thanks," I said.

"Do you need anything?" he asked.

"We were just curious why we were still number two doubles," Nathan said.

"We aren't here to argue or anything, just wondering," I added.

"Okay, you have a right to ask. I just felt that your victory, although it was nice and tough was too close to call. Like if you guys had won 6-2 or 6-3 it would have been a no brainer. But one really close victory didn't show me that you guys were clearly better just maybe came up with some better shots at crucial moments," he said.

"So can we challenge them again?" Nathan asked.

"Absolutely," James said, "look, you guys and them are very close. Like I myself don't even know who's better right now."

There was a moment of silence.

"All right guys. Go support Rafael and them. Those guys are in some tough matches right now," James said.

The task seemed straightforward enough. Just beat them again in a more convincing fashion and we would have the number one doubles spot locked up.

BEFORE NATHEN AND I could challenge them the next week, I had to play a singles challenge match against Sean. Sean was on the number three doubles team, and didn't even ask to challenge me, but the coach told us to play a match.

Sean was a good friend, and made some friendly conversation with me before the match.

"How about this Daniel. We'll just say you won 7-5," he said.

"Ha-ha who knows. You'll probably beat me," I said.

Fifteen minutes later, I was down 3-0.

The lights on the court suddenly went off, making it impossible to continue play for at least twenty minutes. I went to gather myself and attempt a comeback but it would be tough. I just wasn't playing that poorly. Sean was just playing great. He was probably the fastest on the team, but had inconsistent shots. Tonight however, he was incredibly consistent, and I couldn't get many points off him at all.

After the lights came on, I struggled to hold serve but got on the board with my first game. He held easily and then broke me easily. I was down 5-1 and had to break him.

After three or four match points for him, I finally evened it up at 5-5. I went on the win 7-5, just like he predicted. I felt bad for Sean. He really deserved to win the match because he played really well but was incredibly proud of myself for coming back to win that match. Sean was ranked right under me, so I guess the result is indicative of our skills.

The next day at practice, I asked James to challenge Ronald who was ranked one spot above me. I was denied but didn't look into it as much since the courts were already full.

In Nathan and Daniel vs. George and Dylan II, we won 6-1. But we still were number two doubles at the next match. I began to get irritated. James had previously said that a 6-2 win would be a clear indicator that Nathan and I were a better doubles team. We had just won 6-1 and yet James did not make good on his word. Nathan and I were both upset about this but did not complain before the match. We talked to each other and agreed that if we went out and put a beat down on our opponent, and did so in a manner in which everyone can see, that James would maybe notice and realize that he had made a mistake.

We went out and smashed aces, smoked passing shots, and hit severely angled volleys for the entire match while yelling and celebrating the whole time.

However, after another dominating win, James did not seem to be impressed by our efforts. While watching the rest of our teammates finish up their matches, Nathan and I did not talk to James at all. In fact, we ignored him for the rest of the way home.

The following day, I asked to challenge Ronald again, but again he wouldn't let me. I got even more irritated. Ronald was ranked two spots above me and I was allowed to challenge him based on John's original rules, but whenever I asked to challenge someone ranked above me, James would instead ask me to play someone ranked below me.

Instead of having me challenge Ronald, who was only ranked one spot above me, he had Dmitri, a freshman, play against George who was seven spots higher than Dmitri. That wasn't supposed to be allowed.

During one late practice, James Bake had me and Nathan play the number three doubles team which now consisted of Tim and Ronald since Sean had gotten injured. Tim and Ronald played well and we messed around just a little bit too much and lost 6-3.

For the first time in the year, we played number three doubles.

However, we were allowed to challenge Dylan and George again. This time we won 6-3. We had beaten them three out of three times but we were still assigned to play number two doubles. I didn't like it.

Why was I going to practice and working so hard just so that I could win my challenge matches and not be rewarded for it?

The coach made me play Christopher in a pro-set which was first to win eight games. I beat Christopher 8-6 after being down 5-0. I couldn't figure out why I was always falling behind early.

After Dmitri beat George he took George's spot. One win took him from twelfth on the depth chart to fifth. When asked to give a reason, Coach Bake said that he had some impressive "losses" and the victory against George solidified Dmitri as a really good player.

I couldn't believe it.

AFTER A MATCH against Wayne, which was by a million miles the best team in the league, Nathan and I joked around. We had lost 6-2, 6-1, which wasn't that poor of a showing compared to other results. We headed for the snacks and began to eat some of the chips that parents had brought for us.

"What are you guys doing?" James asked, "You just got your behinds whipped and now you're all giggling and eating. Shouldn't you be thinking about how poorly you just played and what you could have done better?"

James stormed off.

"What was that?" I asked Nathan.

"Yeah. We didn't play that poorly. Everyone loses to Wayne," Nathan said.

"Whatever," I said.

I put the food down and leaned against a fence to watch Dylan and George play their doubles match. A few feet away, Omar and Rafael were having a conversation with a couple of the girls from the girls' team.

"Guys stop being so loud!" James said, "They're playing a match over there."

I was by myself, a good six or seven feet away. He couldn't have been talking to me, I thought.

But a hand touched my shoulder. It was James' hand. He grabbed me away from the fence.

"What are you doing?" I asked.

"Don't talk when other people are playing a match. It's disrespectful," he said sternly.

"I wasn't talking?!" I yelled, "Why do you always blame me for everything. Get off me for once!"

I stormed away. James came after me and yelled after me. I didn't care. I walked straight ahead without turning around. I really could not stand him anymore. I didn't want to be on the team anymore.

THE NEXT DAY, I told the Athletic Director, who was also my PE teacher about my displeasure with James.

The result was not as I expected. I should have known that the AD would take the side of the coach but I thought that maybe she would understand where I was coming from. It seemed like she did not hear a single thing I said about the coach's favoritism and unfair treatment of not only me but other people on the team as well. She immediately began to ask me questions about whether I gave 100% effort of every moment of every practice and when I honestly answered that I didn't, she began to tell me anecdotes of her husband who played high school football and baseball and how he never missed practice and always gave a full effort. I left the encounter disappointed because my points were not taken and I came out looking like a whiny player who did not want to work hard.

I did not go to practice for about three days afterward, but Nathan convinced me to come back to practice because there was a match coming up.

I went to practice the next day and my teammates all welcomed me back. I did the warm-up running with the team and got myself all sweaty. I thought James would talk to me and try to settle things down but after the runs it didn't seem like he wanted to talk to me. However, while the team was stretching together, he made a few comments about the lack of effort on the team and took some not so subtle shots at me. Just when everyone was about to begin practice, James pulled me aside and asked me if there was anything I wanted to say to him. I began by telling him pretty much the same thing I told the Athletic Director. He got mad immediately and told me how he knew about me talking to the Athletic Director and that he did not appreciate me getting him fired. He also told me he expected me to say sorry instead of repeating what I said already to the Athletic Director. I tried to explain that I was not trying to get him fired. I was just unhappy with the team and the coach and that it was my right to speak to the Athletic Director about that. He then demanded that I go home and that my dad come apologize to him.

I told my dad about what I had done and he wasn't very happy with me. He told me that he did not think

I should quit the team and that I should try to solve the problem within the system. He said that talking to the Athletic Director was definitely what made the Coach mad because few if any student athletes ever went to that extreme a measure when they had a problem with their coach.

My dad also advised me to try to solve the problem by apologizing first without getting him involved. I called James and gave sort of a half-hearted apology because I still believed what I said. I made sure to tell him that I was not trying to get him fired and that I was sorry for the distraction I brought to the team and that I was sorry for any misunderstanding.

He called me back soon after and said that he welcomed me back to the team.

However, I didn't play in the two remaining tennis matches that season. It felt like some sort of punishment. I reported something that I thought was unfair and did not violate any rules, but almost directly because of my reporting of the matter, I got punished, unfairly.

At that point, I had already made up my mind not to join the tennis team the next year. When tennis season came around for my junior year, I stayed true to me decision and did not join the team. However, I wasn't going to stop playing tennis.

A the beginning of tennis season of my junior year James asked me several times to play, but I had made up my mind to stayed true tom y decision.

That explains why I was on a tennis court that Wednesday afternoon.

Chapter Six

MY MOM WAS not home yet, so I walked upstairs to my room directly.

I sat in front of my desk, opened up my laptop without thinking. When I was about to click the Google Chrome browser I started realized that I needed to write the letter to the Principal that my had asked for.

I began to think back about what happened. It was all very clear in my mind, and I can almost remember every single detail of my interaction with Fred, Harrison, Coach James, and all of my friends and classmates. However, my hands simply could not move to type any words.

The conversation with Mrs. Bush also kept playing in my head. Obviously, she or someone else searched and collected and then submitted all that evidence against me within hours after I reported that Fred hit me. Maybe somebody had been monitoring my online activities for a long time. Harrison must have reported the online conversation about two months ago. But how could Mrs. Bush consider that as cyberbullying since it was a two way communication. Harrison modified the screenshot so that it looks like I was doing the dirty talking and he was a victim so I knew that I needed to find that exchange online so that I could present the real uncensored thing to prove that it was not bullying.

It was an easy task to find the screenshot. I looked at it. I remembered correctly, Robin had started a status poking a small joke on me. Harrison then called me a loser and that started everything. With this evidence, I can prove that Harrison was trying to frame me up which is in fact worse than saying bad words. "It doesn't matter what you say anymore. The decision has been made and you are suspended for two days." As I thought about how I could use the screenshot to prove that I did not bully Harrison, Mrs. Bush's words were circling in my head.

I was extremely angry when I recalled my conversation with Mrs. Bush. And at this point in time, if I saw her, I could have ripped her head off and felt no remorse. I felt an extreme anger that I rarely ever felt. When I was angry at people before, I never thought I would kill them. I wanted to kill Mrs. Bush. I fantasized about spiking her coffee with acid. It's not like I haven't fantasized about beating the pulp out of somebody before, but when I imagine them all bloody (and this is assuming that I could pull off such a thing) I would feel sorry. When I imagined Mrs. Bush all bruised and bloodied from my fists and feet I felt zero remorse. I hated her.

A FEW PERCENT of my brain cells forced me to come back to the reality. I needed to write to the principal to appeal the suspension. Did I really have a chance to appeal?

I first forgot about appealing the suspension, I wanted to prove that if what I did was a crime then everyone in the school was as guilty as I was.

I quickly logged onto Facebook and started collecting Facebook inputs of other students. It's not difficult at all to find something that is juicier than what Mrs. Bush collected against me:

Have never hated someone so much in my whole entire life than I hated Kelly. No one knows how crazy bitch is. Seriously.

The soccer team captain wrote:

Fahge, S the D

There was a sarcastic fan page of the on-campus Policeman and many sarcastic fan pages of other teachers at school. One of the most hated teachers was the AP Chemistry teacher and there was no shortage of displeasure toward this particular teacher.

After only fifteen minutes of searching, I found many pieces of evidence that showed that what I did, though wrong, was something that most people in High School did. In fact, the people who posted crazy or mean things online probably outnumbered the students who didn't.

As I was printing out pages and pages of Facebook screenshot, my mom called me to come eat dinner so I slowly walked downstairs.

ON SATURDAY MORNING, my mom knocked the door to wake me up. I sat up on the bed and my head still felt very heavy, I did not remember when I had fallen asleep, after saving many pages of Facebook screenshots.

I need to write what happened for my dad, I thought. I have to take a shower.

I sit down at my desk and about to write. Dad came in asking me whether I had write up anything,

"I'm working on it."

"OK. I want you to write down every detail, you understand?"

"Yes, I will." I answer without showing any emotion.

Before my dad leaving the room, my thought drifted away from what I suppose to write. How could they punishment based on what I did outside school. This is a gross violation of my first amendment right. I need to challenge this suspension based on the Constitution. Yes, I need to contact the law professor at UC Berkeley from whom I took law lesson last summer.

The email was out within a minute. But I don't know whether he would read and respond. I had no contact with him after last summer's class at Berkeley.

Even he did not respond, I will do it by myself.

As I type "First amendment right, high School student" into Google search bar, a lot of hit come up. Sure, this is not a new topic, and there are a lot of discussions on this.

What I said online may be awful, but the first amendment right is there to protect speeches that are controversial. If the contents are not controversial, then everybody will accept, and therefore there is no need of first amendment right protection.

I spent most morning of Saturday searching and studying the first amendment right for high school students. The review article written by Brandon J. Hoover seems most relevant to my case. Based on this article, before the internet age, it seems there is a clear distinguish between what is inside school and what is not. But now, with all the online activities it is not straightforward to use the precedent to make a judgment.

All I need to do is to prove that all the evidence against me was out of school.

But I already told that to Mrs. Bush. "It's in school now." Mrs. Bush's words ring in my ears.

There are several cases at court pending trial. But the Superior Court has not weighed in on this issue.

Going to the Superior Court? Why not? I will go to anywhere to prove my innocent.

But wait, why on the earth do I have to prove my innocent? To the school, to my parents? Is it the fundamental idea of this country that everyone is innocent until proven guilty? How come it became guilty until proven innocent for me?

For the whole Saturday and morning of Sunday I basically switch between considering how to fight the suspension all the way to the superior court and collecting online evidences of other students. My parents checked me from time to time asking whether I had finished the writing. But gradually I can notice the expression of their eyes was more concern than mad at me.

AFTER THE DINNER, my parent called me into the study. I handed them a two page write up about what happened. My dad read it quickly and then put it on the desk: "What is your thought about this suspension and what is your plan?"

"It's not fair." My answer is as short as it can be.

"Daniel, we noticed you were extremely upset, and your behaviors over the weekend worried us, a lot. We are also very upset about it, you know, your dad almost had an accident on the freeway on the way to school on

Friday. Right now we want you know that no matter what happened we love you and will help you to overcome whatever consequences from this suspension." My mom said, with tears in her eyes.

"Although what you told us does not make sense to us, and it's hard for us to believe that the school use online information of more than one year old to punish you, we are willing listen to your story, and want to help you to get out of this mess, quickly. You need to tell us the truth so that we can work together to find s solution that is best for you. No matter what actually happened, this is a hard lesson for you, and at the end of the day you need to get something positive from this." My dad added.

I did not say anything, but I clearly sensed that their attitude had changed over the weekend. Although they still did not fully believe me, at least they want to hold their judgment and try to find what actually happened. Instead of simply blaming me for doing stupid things and lecturing me what I should do, they are now talking about helping me and finding solutions.

Both my parent are highly educated. They gave me a comfortable home and good learning opportunities. However, I never had a chance to argue with them for almost everything. For whatever I did they were quick to reach a verdict, which in most case is that what I did was plainly wrong or stupid.

"I knew I did something stupid, but still it is not fair." This time I used the "stupid" first.

My dad picked up the two page write-up, and asked:" Are you sure that all you wrote here are true?"

"Yes", I said without hesitate.

"OK, then you need to write a detailed version, What you wrote here is just an outline for what happened, but

I want you to write every details. Who said what at what time etc.?" My dad said.

"We will send an email to the principal asking to postpone the suspension so that we would have time to understand what actually happened. You had told us what happened, but if you really believe that the suspension was not fair, you need to write down all the details so that we can discuss with the school." My mom added.

It's a surprise to me that my parents would trying to delay the suspension instead simply punishing me. But obviously they were not convinced that I was wrongly accused and punished. I need to prove my innocent to them, but at least they gave me the benefit of doubt.

I went back to my room, starting writing down a chronicle of what happened from Wed to Friday. At about ten o'clock, my parent called me to the down study again. Apparently they have been in the study the whole evening. I am not sure what they were doing but they both have a serious look.

"We are going to send this email to the principal, and just want you to have a look." My mom said.

I sit down at the chair to read the computer screen.

April 4th, 2010

Dear Mr. Fahge,

We are parents of Daniel Liu. The purpose of this email is to ask you to postpone the suspension of Daniel so that we would have a little more time for communications and discussions regarding the incident happened on April 1st, 2010 which leads to the suspension. The followings are the main reasons that we make this request:

1. *The wellbeing of Daniel. We are deeply concerned about Daniel's reaction to this suspension decision. As we all understand that whenever facing punishment the kid will always try to find excuses, defend himself and even deny, but by observing his behavior and looking into his eyes we can figure out deep in his heart whether or not he believe that he deserves the punishment. The re action we observe so far convinced us that if this suspension is implemented as planned it will have profound and extremely negative impact on his education in the school and his long term development.*

2. *The purpose of education. We have no doubt that you will agree that ultimate goal of everything the school does, including disciplinary measure, is to educate the students and making them a better human being. We can firmly tell you that if this suspension is implemented as planned, it will not serve the well intended objective, and instead it will cause severe damage to him that nobody wants to see. If you could postpone this suspension action to allow a little more time for communications and discussions, then final outcome would serve the education purpose much better.*

3. *No obvious negative effect. We cannot see any negative impact on school education if this suspension is postponed. Of course, there is always a possibility that you have some other concerns t hat we are not aware of.*

We would like to emphasize that we appreciate the prompt actions you have taken to bring a conclusion and solution to this incident and we want to work together with school to make the education process work. However, currently we cannot convince Daniel that the punishment is fair and is a good learning experience for him. We believe taking a little more time to communicate and discuss will make the education process much more effective and meaningful and will r educe the negative impact. Therefore, we respectively ask you to postpone the suspension.

We will appreciate very much if you can consider our request and make the decision as soon as possible. We will be at school before ~7:30 am on Monday, April 5, 2010 and would like to meet you to discuss this. You can also reach us at 413-228-3859.

Thank you very much for your attention and best regards,

Sincerely yours,

Anna Liu
Michael Liu

Obviously, they spent the whole evening to draft this well organized letter.

"Thank you", was all I can say at that moment.

"Go to sleep now, you need to get up early tomorrow." My mom said.

"I have not finished the writing."

"You can work on it later. You did not get much sleep for two days. So go to bed now." My mom said.

Chapter Seven

Monday, first day of suspension

I woke up at 6:30 am on Monday morning as I normally do. I was supposed to be suspended on Monday and Tuesday following the Thursday of the incident, but my parents wanted to persuade the school to postpone the suspension. When I went downstairs I saw my dad was already on the phone to left voicemails to both Mrs. Bush and Mr. Fahge informing them we were on the way to school

We left home the normal time for school and arrive at school at about 7:15. I wasn't allowed to be on the school campus, so he parked about a block away from the school.

My dad went into the school office by himself to see if he could talk with the principal and delay or postpone my suspension until a clearer explanation was given to us.

While my dad was away, I sat in the car apprehensively. I didn't think he had a great chance at postponing the suspension since Mr. Fahge had told me that I was suspended for at least Monday.

I looked out on the gigantic trees on Locklear. I saw the tiny houses that were pretty much the trademark of the town or city I went to school in. Earlier in the morning, the sun had been pretty bright, but now the blue skies gradually dipped behind misty gray clouds.

Occasionally someone biked by the car but I didn't bother to look up. I shifted my position in the car many times but never felt comfortable. I saw that I had brought my Zune with me and began to listen to a podcast of the Tony Kornheiser show to relax myself. It helped a little but the episode I was listening to wasn't particularly filled with joy and laughter. They talked about some serious subjects as well. Every few minutes I would think of how incredulous my situation was. I couldn't really believe that Facebook conflicts could get me into this much trouble.

I was supposed to have emailed Mr. Fahge by now but I really didn't have the willpower to argue with something that seemed to be a battle that could not be won. They didn't accept any of my arguments before why would they accept them now. I wonder if Mrs. Bush actually even heard anything I told her.

About forty minutes later, my dad walked back to the car. He was obviously not happy.

"What happened?" I asked in Chinese.

"Mr. Fahge's secretary told me he was busy and the earliest time he could meet me would be 11:00am. Since I have a meeting at work at 10:00 am, I am not sure I could stay that late. So I asked to meet Mrs. Bush. At beginning I was told she was not in yet and I needed to wait at the attendance office. Later they told me she was outside watching students coming in. After I waited for more than 20 minutes they told me she was at a meeting outside school and therefore won't be at school in the morning." he answered.

He dialed up the superintendent's office and I could hear some of the things he was saying. Apparently he was talking to the secretary.

". . . So what I asked is that they postpone the suspension until a more detailed investigation is given, and nobody at the school can talk to me" I heard my dad say.

My dad went back into the car, "She will call me back after checking with the superintendent."

After about 15 min, the secretary called back telling my dad that since Mrs. Bush was not at school now another assistant principal would be able to talk to my dad and would call my dad's cell phone very soon.

After waiting for about 20 min, nothing happened. So my dad went to the school again to check.

This time it did not take long to see my dad came back. The school secretary told him since the other assistant principal knew nothing about the incident on Thursday and the suspension; it does not make sense to have the meeting.

I could see the frustration on my dad's face. He called his office to cancel his meeting at work, and then dialed the superintendent office again. After several tries he got connected to the secretary again. The secretary promised to check and call back within 5 min. After about 15 min, my dad called again:

"Mrs. Fernandez, I am sorry I have to call you again. I know you are trying to help and I just want to know whether I need to wait." "OK, I will wait for your call then".

After the phone call, my dad drove to the school district's office, which was only about a three minute drive. "She told me the superintendent would be able to talk to me shortly, so we just go the school district office to see whether we would be able to meet her."

He parked right in front of the building. The secretary called back and connected my dad to the superintendent.

"Can we meet, I'm right in front of your building right now," he said.

". . . okay, I understand. Thank you," he said and hung up.

"Okay," he said to me, "We're going back to the school."

"Why?"

"The superintendent says she will be at school at 11:00 am and we will meet her and the principal at school.

It's about ten o'clock now, so we have to wait about an hour. We drove to the town library so that my dad can check his email using the free Wi-Fi there.

"Mr. Fahge already sent me an email". My dad handed his laptop to me.

Good morning.

With all respect, I told Daniel that he needed to write his appeal to me, to bring evidence of his innocence that had not been presented to Mrs. Bush earlier. Instead of being angry at the whole situation, that is what he should have done. Until it is, then his suspension stands. Please keep him at home and have him write the detail I've requested.

Thank you.

Andrew Fahge
Principal
Chester High School

Again, he asked me to prove my innocent. They randomly picked up some information online to accuse me and then asked me to prove my innocent.

My dad drove in silence toward to school. I didn't really have anything to say either. It's getting warm outside, so after getting to the school, my dad parked in a spot under a big tree about a block away and got out of the car again, leaving me sitting there with my own thoughts.

A long time passed, maybe thirty minutes. My dad finally came back.

"What happened this time?" I asked.

"He still did not agree to postpone the suspension."

"What did he said then?"

"Just the same things he said to you. That he wants you to write him an email and the appeals process can go from there," he said.

"Oh," I said, "What do we do now?"

"It's OK he did not agree to postpone. I got a firm answer from him, that's what I need. He also promised to review the case."

Although he said it's OK, my dad was obviously frustrated by the receptions he experienced this morning.

"Although I'm fighting for you now and I'm saying only things that make you seem more innocent, I'm only saying that to them. To you I have to tell you that what you did is incredibly stupid. You are not without fault here. Do you understand?"

"Yes,"

"Never do something this stupid again. If someone makes fun of you, so what? Leave it alone. Now that you don't leave it alone and always fight back you get into this kind of trouble," he said.

"I'm sorry," I said.

"I cancelled a meeting this morning. It wasn't just any meeting. It was a meeting to discuss the next fiscal year and for me to present what I'm going to work on this upcoming year. It was hard to schedule this meeting, it was with a guy that not anyone can get a meeting with. So you must understand how much I have personally sacrificed to help you." He Said.

"Yes," I said.

We were on the highway now. The weather was in great parallel with my mood for the day. The gray clouds were endless and not much sunlight was permitted through them. Dark and moody.

"Do you think what we're doing is worth it?" he asked me.

"Yes, I really don't agree with what they've done and how they made their decision," I said.

There wasn't much conversation throughout the rest of the trip home. He just sighed occasionally.

He pulled up on the driveway with one final sigh, "When will you grow up and start being more smart?" he asked, "don't do anything stupid anymore."

I got out of the car in silence and got inside the house.

AT ABOUT 4:30 in the afternoon, both my parent was back home. I heard them talking loudly so I went downstairs to see what happened.

Both of them were still standing in the living room, looked very upset.

"We just came back school after meeting the principal." My dad said.

"You met with him again?"

"Yes, I received an email from Mr. Fahge at about 2:00 o'clock saying he already reviewed the case, and would like to meet us to show the evidences, so we went to school to meet him." My dad handed me a folder.

I open it up, on top is a printout of Mr. Fahge's email:

April 5th, 2010

Dear Mr. Liu,

Thank you for coming in this morning to meet with me.

As I said I would do, I have reviewed all of the documentation collected by Mrs. Bush during her lengthy investigation of the conflict reported last week between Daniel and some other Chester High School students. I have significant evidence of cyber-bullying conducted by Daniel towards two different students, some of which provoked the physical altercation between Fred Guo and Daniel on Thursday. I also have evidence that Daniel was involved in the temporary theft of Fred's cell phone and headphones after school on Wednesday which is part of the pattern of harassment and bullying perpetrated by Daniel towards other students.

As you may know, it is now a crime in California to cyber-bully which is defined by the National Crime Prevention Council as "when the Internet, cell phones or other devices are used to send or post text or images intended to hurt or embarrass another person." We take this crime very seriously, as I am sure you do, and want to use appropriate means to bring an end to this ugly misuse of electronic communication systems

I want to point out that I have asked repeatedly for Daniel to write to me and make me aware of any new information not already provided to Ms. Bush that might help me determine his innocence in this matter. I asked him to do so on Friday afternoon, I wrote the same to you in an email this morning, and then asked you to require that of him when I met you later this morning. I have not yet received any such email from Daniel.

I have copies of some of the evidence which I can provide to you along with the actual suspension document. The suspension document will also be mailed to you. Please set up an appointment to come in and view the evidence I have available for you.

Thank you for your patience and please contact me if you have any questions.

Sincerely,

Andrew Fahge
Principal
Chester High School

Under that, they are three pieces evidences against me. One is the screenshot of my Facebook status on Wednesday, March 31st with my dialog with George about Fred.

George had made the comment about Fred overreacting to what was a harmless prank by threatening to "kick his ass" and getting the parents involved unnecessarily. I had agreed with George about not letting Fred bring both of us down over something this petty.

Another is also a screenshot of a Facebook page. It contains the picture of tennis team, and from left to right went Ronald, Josh, Dylan, George, me, Nathan, Fred, Sean, Omar, Rafael. On the lower part of the page, there were comments from several people, including me, made on March 24th, 2009:

George Tang: I'm in the center baby!

Omar: Gangster XXX Tang

George Tang: Damn i have chinky eyes. w8 think i was blinking. my eyes closed are as big as nathan's open.

Daniel: "U got UR leg cross, U R gay".

And the third piece is a print of my Twitter account input on July 2009, eight months before all of this took place.

"Is this the same evidence that Mrs. Bush showed to you last Friday?" My dad asked.

"She showed me more. There is a print out of urbandictionary.com, a screenshot of Facebook status accusing me cyberbully Harrison. I believe that was the dialogue I had with Harrison about two month ago but with most of Harrison's comments were removed so it looks like I was doing monologue. She just flipped in front of me but won't allow me to really look at it. But I am sure that is from that online dialog, just after the Winter Olympics."

"Seems like they did not show us all the evidence." My dad said.

"Whatever he already showed us must be the strongest evidences they have." My mom said.

"These are the strongest evidence they have to punish Daniel for cyberbullying? I can't believe it." My dad seems pretty upset.

"Well, he said they have more, including the testimonies from other students they could not show us." My mom said. "However I am not convinced that he really has more damaging evidence against Daniel. It seems to me that he was trying to scaring us away. He does not look like a nice person at all, and was pretty arrogant at the beginning." My mom said.

"But he must have realized we were pretty serious about this. He obviously did not carefully review the case. When we pointed out that tennis team picture on Facebook was more than one year old, he was genuinely surprised. And when we talked about the phone call from Fred, he admitted that he was not aware of it." My dad said.

"Mrs. Bush did not even check with Josh although I told her that Fred used Josh's phone to make the call." I chimed in.

"Well, I showed him the phone record. So he knew we had evidence to prove that phone call did occur, although he continues to argue that we could not prove what Fred said." My dad added.

"He must felt the pressure when we challenged him that why they did not bother to interview Daniel before the suspension. Oh, you interview 10 people to collect evidence again somebody but never bother to interview that person, it just does not make sense." Mom seems still pretty upset.

I certainly can tell the change of attitude of my parent. What they just learned from the principal is consistent with what I told them. It is not what I told them that does not make sense, it is what the school did does make sense.

"Daniel, tell us the truth, have you done any other stupid things?" My dad asked.

"No, I told you everything."

"Have you finished your writing?" Dad asked

"Almost."

"You can see, he showed us some of the evidence they had against you. Some of it is terrible, some of it really is," he said, "But it still doesn't make it fair to punish you. Using some online conversation more than one year old to punish somebody is plainly wrong, and we are not going to take it. This is personal, and we're going to fight it." My dad said passionately.

"Okay," I said, but a little surprised by my dad's reaction.

"Are you willing to stick with this and try to get your suspension appealed?"

"Yes."

"Okay then we're going to fight against it. But it might be tough on you. See, I'm going to have to make sacrifices, your mom will make sacrifices, but it will be the toughest on you," he warned.

"I know," I said.

"From now on you need to keep a record of everything by writing," my dad said.

"Everything?"

"Yes, here is what I wrote down for this morning."

4-5-2010

Arrived at school office at ~ 7:25am. The principal was in the office but after consulting with the principal the secretary told me he was not available but he had reply my email. I did not see the email before I left home. The earliest time he would be available would be 11:00 am, and I asked for a note and she wrote one for me.

I asked for Mrs. Bush but she told me that she did not have her schedule and I need to go to the attendance office.

Nobody was at the attendance office ~ 7:30am, so I went back to main office. The secretary told me that the office is about to open, and actually she just saw Mrs. Bush walked in.

Waiting at attendance office since ~ 7:30am. At ~ 7:50am. I asked whether there is wireless available since I would like to check my email. I was told there no wireless available. The secretary at attendance office told me that Mrs. Bush was not in today so I went back to Main office. Only a student was at the office. Tried consular office where also only a student was there. Went back to attendance office and let the secretary to take a message and left my cell number. Ask her to inform the principal and Mrs. Bush that I am going to contact the school district.

Made phone calls to school district and education board chair. At ~ 8:15am talk to Mrs. Fernandez, She said she will contact the superintendent and probably will be able to back to me at @ 9:00am

8:50 Mrs. Fernandez called me back said the vice principal Tamis will call me soon.

After waiting about 15 min, I did not receive the phone I went to the CHS talk to the main office, ask whether Mrs. Tamis would be able to talk to me. The secretary radio the principal. Few min later Mr. Fahge spoke to me saying he is still busy, Mrs. Tamis did not know the incident. Mrs. Bush is at the meeting. He had to leave and can't talk me any longer. I told him I respect, but as parent I will continue try to work on this.

About 9:30 I went to attendance office asking for a copy of suspension notice and supporting document. I was told without Mrs. Bush she could not find it. She will let Mrs. Bush know when she came back.

I called Mrs. Fernandez again to let her know that I was not able to have discussion with anybody at CHS. She asked me to hold. Then she said she will call me within 5 min. After more 10 min I call Mrs. Fernandez again to see whether I would be able to talk to anybody or not. Since I cannot wait too long. She said superintendent is on the phone, and she did not know when the superintendent could finish the call, but she will let me know as soon as possible. If I did not hear from her in 5 min I can call again. So I drove to school district and wait there. Later at ~ 9:55am she call me and transfer me to the superintendent. She said that it's a special situation today since Friday was a religion holiday, so not everybody was at school so Mrs. Tamis was not at school on Friday. To have a meaningful discussions I have to talk to Mr. Fahge and Mrs. Bush. She will be at CHS at 11:00am to meet me and Mr. Fahge.

I waited another hour and arrived at CHS office at ~ 10:55am. Mrs. Superintendent arrived at the same time, and we introduced each. She asked me to wait at the main office and then walked into Mr. Fahge's office. I heard Mr. Fahge said that I did not want the 11:00am appointment. A couple min later, Mrs. Superintendent walked out, told me that Mr. Fahge will be with me soon.

Later Mr. Fahge walk out and invited me to his office. The first sentence he said was "I don't understand". There is obvious frustration on his face that I keep trying to talk to somebody at CHS. So I said I would to explain to him what happened so far this morning since there are some misunderstanding. I told him that I called both him and Mrs. Bush and left voicemail this morning before I left home and gave them my cell #. I did not see the email before I left but learn the email content indirectly from my wife. I also felt frustrated since I received a lot conflict info but I can understand that everybody was busy. If for any reason he had hurting feeling I am sorry but all I try to do is to talk to somebody to seek the postpone of the suspension. I tried to tell him that as a father I deeply worry the situation of Daniel, and all I ask now is a postpone so that we will have more time to communicate. He made it clear to me that he declined the request. I told him I respect his decision. He repeatedly said that Daniel needs to email him. We had more discussions about how to help Daniel. He offered to talk to him, but I eventually declined.

THE WHOLE EVENING I was writing the details of what happened since last Wed while my parents were busy collecting information on how to appeal the suspension and looking for lawyers. It is a little surprise to me that they changed attitude and that they seem pretty determined to fight the suspension. The change of attitude of my parents made me felt better since they begun to believe me and were willing to help me to seek justice.

As I was writing, an instant message from Isaac caught my attention:

"I'm scared for u."
"Why?"
"James said some things about you today."
"Like What?"
"He was like, 'Daniel better watch his back when he is alone. If I catch him in a dark corner or something, it's bad for him.'"
"Really? What the hell . . ."
"Yeah, he was pretty mad and he said he might go to your house"

"Wow, he does not know where I live. Why is he even going to come to my house?"

"Fred's mom told him you talked trash about him online."

"When?"

"Today at tennis practice."

I sat on my chair staring at the screen not knowing what I should make of this and what I should do. Fred was at the tennis practice this afternoon, so he was only suspended for one day but I was suspended for two days. I knew Fred's father was a former teacher at the school, and Fred's mom goes to school all the time and is friends with many teachers and officials at school, so I wasn't too surprised that Mrs. Bush favored Fred. But the fact that they punished me more than Fred still made me angry. James Bake was angry at me and wanted to get me. I don't want to watch my back in the dark. If he has any issue with me, he should challenge me or at least come to me up front.

Mrs. Bush could not tell me anything about Fred because she claimed that everything is confidential, but how come Fred's mom knew everything about my situation and spread them at school? I had nothing to do with that Urbandictionary.com stuff, but Mrs. Bush used it to accuse me and even shared it with Fred's mom, or actually it was probably Fred's mom that brought that printout and showed Mrs. Bush. Mrs. Bush then used it without even checking the validity of the accusation. Since I reported that Fred hit me, they had to do something about Fred, but they only suspended him for one day. To justify that, they must prove I was also guilty.

This is retaliation. I felt my spine tingle when I thought about this.

> **"Still there?"**
> "yeah."
> **"What are you going to do?"**
> *"Don't know, wait him to come get me lol."*
> **"Get real man."**
> *"Will u be a witness if I report it?"*
> **"I don't want get into troubles but if have to I will."**
> **"Everybody heard that."**
> **"Be careful, I was really scared."**

I sat there with my mind roaming from raging to depression. I don't care whether James Bake would really hurt me, but how could Mrs. Bush was so in bed with Fred and his mom. Probably I should hit back on Wed. since it really does not matter how I reacted. If the school system was so corrupted is it worthwhile to appeal the case?

I did not realize that my parents walked to my room.

"How are you?" my mom asked. She probably did not really need an answer since the expression on her face told me she knew I was not that good.

I showed them the IM with Isaac, and both of them were quite shocked after reading it.

"What should we do? Should we call the police?" I asked.

"Probably not. At least not now." My dad answered. "James Bake is a pretty nice guy, so I don't think he will really come to our house. Most likely he was just angry after heard the rumor from Fred's mom. If we report this to police now and what Isaac told you was proved to be true, he would be in trouble, most likely be fired as coach. Our goal is to overturn the suspension, and we should try control the situation. But you do need to save these IM messages as evidence. On the other hand, we need to activate the security system at our house just in case." My dad said.

"But this really tells us something." My mom said. "It is outrageous that they only suspend Fred for one day but suspend Daniel two days."

"It seems they work closely. On Monday afternoon when Mrs. Bush called me to tell me that Daniel was hit, at that time she already mentioned that Daniel was provocative and she was still investigating the incident. She called me around four o'clock, that only about three hours after the incident. Oh, no, Daniel, you were at the attendance office since you report the incident and did not leave until 7th period, is that right?"

"Yeah, Mrs. Bush did not talk to me until 7th period." I answered.

"When dose the 7th period start?"

"2:20."

"So, you probably left Mrs. Bush's office between two thirty and three. Let me check my phone record." My dad went online to pull the calling record. "Here you go. She called me at 4:30pm. So in less than two hours she had pretty much made up her mind to punish Daniel. She was very efficient."

"I knew Fred's mom was very familiar with the school, and now seems she was pretty happy and proud with what she was doing." My mom said. "Now we still focus on the appeal, and we will use this evidence when necessary."

"This is a good thing, son." My dad continued, "Now all we ask is Daniel should not be punished more than Fred. If they don't agree, they need to explain why they think Daniel should be punished more."

I am not sure whether my dad really believes this is a positive thing or just wants to calm me down.

Chapter Eight

NEXT MORNING, MY parents left home as they normally do, but they were back home together at about 10:00am. They did not go to work, instead they just had a meeting with a lawyer, Mr. Ralph. He is not specializing on education law and current work for a big company on environmental issue. So he is not really trial lawyer now but as a friend he is willing to give some advices before we hired a lawyer.

When he read the official suspension notice and the three pieces of evidence, he believes it is almost laughable that the school use such web based information to make accusation. If this is a normal civil law suit, they will be laughed out of room. However he indicated the education law is the area he was not familiar with and we should assume the school knows what they are doing. So he needs to do a little research on education law.

"Mr. Fahge already sent us an email." My dad said. Both my mom and I move to the screen to read the email.

April 6th, 2010

Dear Mr. Liu,

I wanted you to know that I spoke with Ms. Bush after our meeting this afternoon. I wanted her perspective about whether she interviewed Daniel as part of the evidence gathering process. She said that she met with him around 2:00 p.m. on Friday and without initially mentioning anything about suspension, she described to him what she had uncovered about the cyber-bullying in order to give him a chance to respond. She describes his response as being very defensive, not listening, and not presenting any new information about what took place. It was after 10 minutes of unproductive conversation that she informed him of the suspension. So, she sees that time as an opportunity for him to have told his side of the story and provide substantive new information.

We have at least 4 different opportunities for Daniel to have provided substantial information about the conflict. First, Thursday after lunch when he informed Mrs. Bush of being hit by Fred; second, on Friday around 2:00 when she told him of the information she had gathered in the day that followed; third, when Daniel approached me on Friday afternoon and I told him to write me an email outlining new information that might help us understand his perspective more; and then again today, when I met with you and urged you to have him write this email (plus I had sent the same request to you via email early this morning). At no point has he given a fully detailed written statement (or verbal for that matter) that might help us understand his perspective on the cyber-bullying issue.

As I said to you earlier, Daniel is invited to contact Ms. Bodder, my secretary, to set up a 1/2 hour meeting to give him one more opportunity to give his perspective. You are welcome to be a part of such a meeting as long as it is understood that he is the one to be giving his perspective.

Sincerely,
Andrew Fahge
Principal
Chester High School

"It is a lot softer than the previous one. He now 'invites' Daniel to present evidence." My dad said after reading.

"He certainly realized they made a lot of mistakes, and now he is trying to find cover." My mom added.

"What do you think?" My dad asked.

"No," I said, "some of it is false."

"What's false about it?" my dad asked.

"First of all, sixth period ends at 2:12 so there is no way I could have started talking to her in her office at 2:00. Also, she told me that I was suspended like three minutes into our conversation. So the rest of the time I was angry while I made my case. And I was not aware that this was a time for me to defend myself," I said. "She shown me the Facebook stuff, and when I tried to defend myself she told me it does not matter what I was saying the decision was already made. She also told me Mr. Fahge already reviewed and agreed. So definitely they made the decision before the meeting." I answered.

"OK, then you need to write a rebuttal. I will forward this email to you." My dad asked. "and we need to respond to Mr. Fahge."

"Right now we just tell them we need a little more time to prepare and we will call again to schedule the meeting. Also we may bring a lawyer." My mom suggested.

"Can we also bring a lawyer for Wednesday morning?" I asked. Before I go back to class there should be a parent conference. Considering what they had done so far, I really do not want to talk to any school official without a lawyer.

"Mr. Ralph is willing to help, I will check with him this afternoon." My mom answered.

After making phone calls to the school, my parents left home to go to work, leaving myself at home to write the rebuttal.

When I back my room, I read the email again. They did not give me a chance to defend myself and now they try to spin facts so that they could protect themselves.

It is not difficult for me to write down what happened on Friday since it is still so vivid in my head. But the hard part is I have to replay that terrible memory. Mrs. Bush's sneer really hurt me. But I have to be focused to write the rebuttal.

About an hour later, I emailed the rebuttal to my parents.

April 6th, 2010

Dear Mr. Liu,

I wanted you to know that I spoke with Ms. Bush after our meeting this afternoon. I wanted her perspective about whether she interviewed Daniel as part of the evidence gathering process. **(It was not a interview. I was never asked to present evidence)**. *She said that she met with him around 2:00 p.m.* **(it is impossible for me to be at attendance office at 2:00pm since the class ended at 2:12)** *on Friday and without initially mentioning anything about suspension, she described* to him what she had uncovered about the cyber-bullying in order to give him a chance to respond. *(**Whenever I tried to defense I was cut off many time**)* She describes his response as being very defensive, not listening, *(**if you want I can give you a detailed description of the conversation**)* and not presenting any new information about what took place *(**She never ask me to present evidence. Before the meeting I have no idea that I was accused of bullying, how could I present any evidence?**)*. It was after 10 minutes of unproductive conversation that she informed him of the suspension. *(**It is definitely much less than 10 min**)* So, she sees that time as an opportunity for him to have told his side of the story and provide substantive new information. *(**With all the authority and resources available the school spent 26 hours prepare the evidence to against me. So 10 min is enough for me to provide substantial new information?**)*

We have at least 4 different opportunities for Daniel to have provided substantial information about the conflict. First, Thursday after lunch when he informed Ms. Bush of being hit by Fred *(**at that time, all we talked is about that I was hit by Fred. Later on, new allegations was brought against me, do you really believe that is an opportunity for me?**)*; second, on Friday around 2:00 *(again this is wrong)* when she told him of the information she had gathered in the day that followed; third, when Daniel approached me on Friday afternoon and I told him to write me an email outlining new information that might help us understand his perspective more *(**Mr. Fahge told me I could only appeal the suspension after I serve the suspension, so this is not an opportunity for me to defense myself**)*; and then again today, when I met with you and urged you to have him write this email *(plus I had sent the same request to you via email early this morning)*.

At no point has he given a fully detailed written statement (or verbal for that matter) that might help us understand his perspective on the cyber-bullying issue

When my parents came home in the evening, the first thing they told me Mrs. Bush had canceled the meeting on Wednesday morning. They showed me the email from Mrs. Bush:

April 6th, 2010

Dear Mr. Liu,

Thank you for your voice message this morning. We do not need to meet, so I am canceling that appointment regarding Daniel's suspension before returning to classes. However, Daniel must meet with Mr. Fahge tomorrow morning before attending classes.

At this point all meetings regarding this incident and Daniel's suspension should be arranged through Mr. Fahge. Also please note that if you are planning to bring a lawyer with you to any meeting, we will need to schedule accordingly so that our attorney is also present.

Thanks,

G. Bush

Greta Bush
Assistant Principal
Chester High School

Obviously, when she learned that we might bring a lawyer to the parent conference on Wednesday morning she canceled the meeting. Although I was happy that I did not need to meet Mrs. Bush again, I also wondered why by just mentioning the lawyer I could avoid the meeting I did not want?

"Tomorrow, you need to first go to Mr. Fahge's office at 7:30am. He wants to talk to you and see how you are doing," my dad said.

"What if I don't want to talk to him?" I asked.

"No, you should. But be careful what you say. You just need to say that you are OK and ready to back to school. If he ask any questions you don't feel comfortable to discussion, just tell him you'd rather to have a separate meeting to discuss. Since he knows that we might bring in a lawyer, I believe he will not ask you specific questions. All he wants to do is to check you status and make sure you are OK to back to school." my dad said.

"Okay," I said. And then asked "Do I have to email Mr. Fahge before returning school tomorrow?"

"No. I had another meeting with Mr. Ralph this afternoon. He did a little study on California Education code, and found that the education code gives school a lot room to maneuver. Although he still believe what school did was unreasonable and professionally questionable, it won't be an easy task to overturn the suspension. For example, the state law did not give specifics on how to appeal a suspension. So the appeal is very much school dependent." My mom says.

That does not seem very exciting, I thought. If the appeal is school dependent, how much chance do I have to overturn the appeal if the law does not specify what they should do?

"I already asked Mr. Fahge for a formal the appeal procedure, here is his answer". My mom showed an email printout.

April 6th, 2010

Dear Ms. Liu,

There are two appeal opportunities. One is for Daniel to write a statement as has been requested both verbally by me to him on Friday, your husband and you yesterday, and in various emails. I will actively consider any new evidence he brings forth, and determine whether it makes a substantial difference in our investigation and conclusion.

The second kind of appeal would be for you to write a letter to Superintendent Megan Anderson describing your disagreement with the decision made by the administration of Chester High School and requesting that she reconsider the case at her level. She would then likely want to meet with Daniel and you and his father and then with the CHS administration before she would make a decision.

Andrew Fahge
Principal
Chester High School

"So they don't have a formal procedure." My dad said.

"Apparently not. That what I got when I asked him for an appeal procedure." My mom answered.

"Then we need to be very careful to avoid any potential procedure error." My dad said.

We will fight with someone who is also making the rules and serve as reference to make calls, will this be a fair game? I thought. I really does not have much confidence of wining the appeal.

"Mr. Ralph will draft a letter on behalf of us to challenge the suspension, and he suggested that we schedule a meeting with the principal and present this letter to him. Although the letter will be signed by us, the principal can definitely recognize that the letter was drafted by a lawyer and therefore know we are working with lawyer and we are serious. Hopefully this will caught his attention and he will review and consider the case more carefully. If he is still very stubborn, we'd better to find an education lawyer because this is really a very special area and we will have a tough battle."

Listening my parents talking about this, I was wondering why on the earth is the lawyer so important? Why don't people just be honest? Why was the law written in such a complex and ambiguous language so that nobody can really understand it unless they spend fifty thousand a year on law school? I could not remember who said the following and obviously it is true, sadly:

"A jury consists of twelve persons chosen to decide who has the better lawyer."

Chapter Nine

MY DAD DROVE me to the school on Wednesday morning. Although I wanted to remove the suspension, I was not eager to go back to school. It wasn't that I was afraid of anything, but there was also nothing I looked forward to. My parents and Mr. Ralph told me that since I was still in the process of appeal with the possibility to go through legal process, I have to "shut up" at school. In fact, even without the consideration of potential legal consequences, I don't think I would talk to anybody about this. How many people would be able to understand me? Whom I can trust? This incident would forever change my perspective of who are friends and how much trust I can bestow upon them.

Mrs. Bush told me she interviewed ten people during the investigation and her decision was based on those statements. Although I do not know the exact list of those 10 people I can pretty accurately guess who they are. Some of them are the witness I brought into the situation. Most of them I considered to be my friends, and quite close friends. What did they say about me in front of Mrs. Bush? I would think most of them definitely like me more than Fred or Harrison. But after experienced that happened in the past few days now I have to ask myself whether what I believed is true. If they were my friends and liked me, how could Mrs. Bush so quickly reached the decision to suspend me, more than Fred? They are two possibilities, those I considered friend did not support me or even betrayed me for some reason, or Mrs. Bush distort whatever they said to justify her decision to punish me in order to protect Fred. Neither of these two scenarios is very encouraging.

We were driving on interstate I-80 toward San Francisco during a typical early morning rush hour. The traffic is slow but not too bad. Some drivers kept trying to switch lanes to make a slight gain of speed. I remembered one example about trust is driving on highway. In order to drive on highway, you have to put a lot of trust on many things you do not necessarily know or have control. You have to trust you car works properly, the brake will work when you are getting too close to the car in front of you; the steering will respond when you want to change lane or make turns. You can do your best to maintain your car so you can trust it, but this only half of the equation. You have to trust many cars around you and the people drive them without knowing anything about the cars or the people. It is not a trust, it's is a blind faith.

How much faith do I have in school and the people in charge of it? I don't know. What I know is in order to survive I have to have at least some faith.

On the way to the school my dad repeatedly told me what I should do at school, such as do not discuss the incident with anyone, stay away from Fred and Harrison, do not get even close to the tennis court etc. I wasn't paying too much attention to his talking, and most of the time I just stared at the cars around us.

My dad parked the car in front of the school. "OK, you go to the principal office directly, just saying that you are ready to go back school, OK? I am pretty sure all he wants to do is to check your status and make sure you are OK to go back to your class. If in case he wants to discuss the incident, you just ask to call me. But I don't think that would happen."

"OK".

"It should be a very short meeting. After the meeting you can borrow the office to call me and let me know you are OK. I will wait here." My dad said.

"I can use my cell phone." I said.

"But I think cell phone use is not allowed during school hour." My dad said.

"Yeah, but I can find a place to make the call, everybody does that."

"No, now you need to be extremely careful. Don't do anything that is not allowed no matter how many other students do it." My dad insists.

"OK." I answered and walked out of the car.

I walked into the main office on Wednesday morning.

"Hi, can I help you?" asked Mrs. Gomez.

"I have a quick appointment with Mr. Fahge this morning," I said.

"Okay, I'll go ask him if he's ready," she said.

"He's just about ready. He's just chatting with a teacher right now," she said after she came out of his office.

I saw my history teacher Mr. DePaul walk of his office smiling.

"Hi Mr. DePaul," I said as he walked out of the main office.

He rolled his eyes and ignored me completely. That was weird, I thought, normally Mr. DePaul always smiles and tells me good morning.

"Daniel, come on in!" Mr. Fahge called.

I walked in slowly and sat down in a chair in front of his desk. I had no intention of staying in there for more than two minutes so I didn't even take my backpack off.

"How are you doing?" he asked.

"I'm fine," I said.

"Good, is there anything that you would like me to know?"

"Nope, not that I can think of right now."

"Come on, there must be something, how do you feel about being back at school?" he asked.

"I'm glad to be back," I said.

"Are you worried about anything?"

"No, not really,"

"Come on, nothing?"

"Well, the course selection sheets are due today and I was supposed to get them signed off by my teachers the last two days and I haven't been able to do that," I said.

"Oh, well we'll be sure to make an exemption for you and let you turn them in a little bit later," he said.

"Thanks," I said.

"If there is anything that makes you feel uncomfortable, you come seeing me immediately."

"Thanks."

"All right," he said as we both stood up, "Go get 'em."

AFETR WALKING OUT of the office, I walked to History class. I was again one of the first people in the classroom. As I walked to my seat, I said, "Hi Mr. DePaul," again.

This time he gave me a little nod of acknowledgement but went to the front of the classroom to organize some things.

People slowly started to come into the room. Most people seemed to know what had happened to me.

"What happened?" asked Parth.

"Uh, I don't really want to talk about it. It's a long story," I said.

"Come on, everyone's talking about it. I just want to know if what people are telling me is true," he said.

"Why don't you just not believe anything, that way everyone's happy," I said.

Right after those words landed, another friend, Timothy asked me about it.

"Did you get suspended?"

I nodded.

"Want to tell me about it?" he asked.

"Not really, sorry," I said.

"Oh, that's fine," he said.

"Thanks for understanding," I said.

"Yeah," he said, "no problem."

I was really wondering why Mr. DePaul was so cold to me today. I had just had a nice discussion with him a week ago about how I could do better in his class and thought that I had gotten on his good side.

I got the answer about twenty minutes later.

"Guys, I'm really disappointed with these essays," he said as he leaned on his teaching stand, "I told you guys in the beginning of the year that you would be writing a lot of essays and you guys got better at it. But on these essays you guys did terribly. It's quite obvious that many of you just did not put the effort into these essays. A few of you guys wrote great essays, but I'm really disappointed with most of your efforts. Helen, how much time did you spend on your essay?"

"No less than five, I didn't exactly keep track," she answered.

"Hear that? That's the kind of time you should be spending on these essays. Some of you guys had really weak theses, some didn't give me enough evidence to back up your thesis. Just all around guys, I'm really disappointed. It's near the end of the year. In college, this is all you'll be doing. You're going to be writing non-stop. That's how work is done after high school. When you guys get jobs, you're going to be writing. Writing things that are much more difficult than what I'm asking of now. So I'm going to pass these out now, and I'm warning you, not a lot of you are going to like the grade you got," he said.

As he walked around the room passing out the essays I was a little bit worried about my own essay. My mind had been focused on so much other stuff that I kind of forgot how my essay was. I know that it wasn't great but wasn't expecting a bad grade.

Suddenly my essay appeared before my eyes held by the extended arm of Mr. DePaul.

"You ask me how to do better in this class and ask me how to get better scores on essays and you give me this. There's not even a works cited page," he said bitterly.

"I footnoted it, I didn't know that—"

"Why don't you spend more time on your essays instead of doing all that online stuff? And I know you know what I'm talking about. And don't get your dad and come harass my ass about how to help you in this class when all you're doing is wasting your time online," he said angrily.

"God damn . . ." said Timothy after Mr. DePaul walked away.

"Don't worry about it man," Timothy said.

"Thanks," I said.

Throughout the day, I was wondering how Mr. DePaul knew about my situation. I knew that the students probably all talked about it a lot. But Mrs. Bush told me that the reasons of my suspension would be kept confidential. Had they violated their own rules? I asked myself. But I had no intention of going to fight with them about it.

When I went to Biology and Journalism, I checked to see what the other teachers were responding to my presence. None of them confronted me or treated me any different. But I still felt like they were looking down on me.

Although even account for the two weekend days I was out of school for 4 days, I felt I was in an unfamiliar place. I need to be constantly alert to what happens around me. I need to carefully watch what I was saying because it might be used later to against me. Everybody's face seems a little stranger to me.

Chapter Ten

"DANIEL," MY MOM said, "Your dad and I talked to Mr. Ralph again today. He says that we should have a pretty good case."

"He also said that what you did is terrible and that the things you said on Facebook are terrible. It is really awful what you said. When we read it, we didn't think that such words could come from you," my dad added.

"You need to stop using this kind of language," my mom demanded sternly, "It not only shows you in a poor light, it reflects the parents of the child when a child talks like this. I don't use dirty language, your dad does not use dirty language. Why do you use this kind of language? Where did you learn this?"

I had no answer. I felt terrible. Once they said that what I did reflected the quality of their parenting, I really felt terrible.

"I'm sorry," was all I could muster.

"Well, Mr. Ralph came up with this. He wrote most of it, but I added some things on it. Take it upstairs to check if everything's correct and edit it if you need to," my dad said as he handed me a stapled two-page packet.

"Hey Daniel, don't let this affect you too much. Make sure your studies are okay, and tell us if you need any help," my mom said.

The packet was two tiny sheets of paper. It probably weighed six tenths of a gram. But as I carried it upstairs it felt like it weighed seventy pounds. The burden of it was way too heavy.

It was probably that moment that I realized the severity of what I had done. Not only did I risk myself, not only did I make a fool out of myself. I made a fool of my parents. Anything I do represents them as much as it represents me. It occurred to me that in the profile of any successful human being, the responsibility of that person's parents is almost always mentioned. Often times we read, "Raised by a single mother" or "raised in a steady two-parent household" or maybe "raised by an alcoholic father".

A person is not only looked at by their own achievements but by what kind of family they came from. A successful person raised by irresponsible parents is seen as someone who is incredibly persevering. A successful person raised by good parents is perceived as someone who has a clear sense of what to do in life. An unsuccessful person raised by good parents is the worst possible scenario. If I wasn't careful, I could easily fall into that much undesired category.

I opened up the folder and started reading the letter.

MICHAEL LIU AND ANNA LIU
1900 Pleasant Hill Drive
Richland, CA 93653

April 8, 2010

Mr. Andrew Fahge
Principal
Chester High School

Re: Initial Appeal of Suspension—Daniel
Liu—Meeting of April 8, 2010

Dear Mr. Fahge,

Thank you for accommodating our initial appeal of the recent two day suspension of our son Daniel Liu. We are pursuing this appeal largely due to the fact that Daniel was physically assaulted by another student while on school grounds. That assault was unprovoked. We were appalled to learn that the instigator of that assault was only suspended for one day while Daniel was suspended for two days. Regardless of the totality of circumstances surrounding this event, something is just plain wrong with the school's decisions in this matter. Nonetheless, we hope to satisfactorily resolve this matter by removing the suspension from Daniel's school record. We are also instituting measures at home to try to ensure that Daniel understands the gravity of this situation so that he can move forward in a positive manner at school.

Daniel followed proper procedures by reporting the assault to school authorities and was subsequently suspended. We find the school's explanation of the evidentiary basis for its suspension decision extremely inadequate. The check-the-box nature of the Official Notice of Suspension makes the form lacking in detail, vague and ambiguous. Our son was assaulted. In no way did his behavior "Disrupt school activities" nor did he defy "valid authority." The notice form goes on to claim that the specific action leading to suspension was "Behavior leading to a fight. Cyber-bullying of another student." As Daniel has explained and will repeat today, he did not take the cell phone or headphones allegedly related to the assault. As explained below, the evidence of "cyber-bullying" provided to us to date is unpersuasive.

The school's use of web based information that is nine months old to insinuate our son has a penchant for stealing headphones is outrageous and provocative. The additional claim that a single year old on-line <u>non-hostile bantering</u> comment regarding a posted picture of the tennis team constitutes "cyber-bullying" is inconsistent with California law.

Finally, the school's justification of its decision with a private on-line Facebook discussion that <u>occurred after school and off school grounds</u> is tenuous at best. <u>It should be noted that the perpetrator of the assault while not a party to that on-line discussion was apparently the instigator of the threats being discussed.</u> In all three examples any conclusion of "cyber-bullying" is fundamentally a misapplication of California law.

Apart from this initial appeal, we are extremely concerned with the continued physical and psychological safety of Daniel while on school grounds. The school's suspension decision has created a negative incentive not only for our son but all students regarding reporting of assaults on school grounds. The impact of that negative incentive cannot be overstated. If Daniel had not reported the assault, he may not have been suspended. If Daniel is assaulted by the same student again and he reports the assault, we are concerned that he will be unjustifiably suspended again. We therefore seek some confirmation that all things remaining the same, Daniel will not be suspended for reporting any such future assaults and that the school will do its best to prevent any further assaults against Daniel.

In the event that we do not satisfactorily resolve this issue today, we would like to know what the process is for an appeal to the School District level.

Very truly yours,

Michael Liu & Anna Liu

I almost laugh after reading the letter, not because it makes very good argument against the evidence the school used to against me, but how the argument was made. I think that what Mr. Ralph was definitely right that the school officials will clearly know that we are working with a lawyer by reading this letter. It may be good that the school will consider the case more seriously, but at the bottom of my heart I still felt uneasy. Why couldn't everyone just be more honest, have more trust, even between students and teachers? I don't know how much my parents need to pay the lawyer, the fact that I need a lawyer to prove my innocent makes me sad.

I returned the letter to my parent downstairs.

"What do you think?" My dad asked.

"Pretty good." I answered.

"We have scheduled a meeting with Mr. Fahge tomorrow at 2:00 pm, and we also asked Mrs. Bush to be there. The main purpose of the meeting is for you to make your case. So you just read from the statement you prepared, and try to avoid answer questions. The only thing we will give them will be that letter." My mom told me.

"Why don't we bring the lawyer?" I asked.

"Since Mr. Fahge requested to have this meeting, so we just assume that he is trying to find a solution, and we certainly hope we could get this issue solved without going through lawsuit. If we bring a lawyer now, we may give them an impression that we have determined to bring a lawsuit against the school, which would make the conversation very unproductive. Don't worry, just sticking to the fact and saying what is true." My mom said.

Chapter Eleven

I WAS CALLED down, again from Spanish class, to principal's office. When I got there Mr. Fahge, Mrs. Bush, and my parents were waiting for me. We had prepared evidence. In a folder, we had many images of people saying things similar to what I said and if it got to that point, we would use the evidence and ask Mr. Fahge what he was going to do about all of these cases of "cyberbullying".

There was also a two page list of reasons why we felt like the suspension was unreasonable.

"Okay," said Mr. Fahge, "Daniel, now that we're all here. Is there anything you have for me or something?"

I took out the list of reasons and began to read them to Mr. Fahge.

"No, no Daniel. Don't read it to me. Can I actually see what you've written?" Mr. Fahge asked.

"Well, this is a rough draft. I didn't prepare anything to actually give to you," I said, "What's the difference between me reading it to you and giving you the copy?"

"I can read faster, and I specifically asked Daniel many, many times that he needed to write something for me. That would be the first step of the appeal process." he said.

"Here," my dad said, "We have prepared a letter on behalf of Daniel that you can have."

My dad extended a two page letter they had prepared toward Mr. Fahge. He took it and put it face down on his desk.

"Thank you, that's great. But I want the writing from Daniel. That's what I've asked for this entire time."

"Let Daniel give him the rough draft." My mom said.

"No." My dad said firmly. "You asked for this meeting to discuss the suspension, but now you insist to have a written statement?"

"Well, considering how contentious the situation is, I have to." Mr. Fahge said.

"Daniel can give you a written statement later." my dad said.

"Oh, okay. Than this meeting is over," Mr. Fahge said as he threw his hands up with disgust.

"Why can't we just discuss the things orally?" I asked, "I don't see why—"

"Why have you not prepared anything in writing?" Mr. Fahge said, "We can reschedule an appointment when you write something that you can give to me."

"I think we have a misunderstanding about the purpose of this meeting. You requested the meeting to give Daniel the opportunity to present his case, but now you insist to have a written statement. I am OK with that. I do want point out that as parents all we are doing is trying to control the situation." My dad said.

"Then we have the same goal." Mr. Fahge said.

"I hope so. I would like to let you know that something is happening that is beyond what school can handle. Somebody already issued a specific threat to Daniel and myself." My dad said, with a lot of emotion.

"Really?" Both Mr. Fahge and Mrs. Bush seem to be surprised.

"Daniel, you can tell Mr. Fahge what you have heard without mentioned any names."

"I had heard from more than persons somebody said 'Daniel'd better to watch his back . . .', and "I will . . . his dad'". I stated.

"Then you should report to police." Mr. Fahge said, looking serious.

"Well, we are monitoring the situation and have not decided whether to report to the police. Obviously, somebody spread the rumor based on the false accusation against Daniel. Again, we want to work with school to get this issue solved, but thing can go ugly if it was not handled properly." My dad added.

"I had talked to each students involved in this incident and ask them not to discuss at school and not to try to take advantage from the situation." Mrs. Bush said, with a calm voice.

It's the first time that I heard Mrs. Bush's voice since last Friday. She seems like a different person now.

"We appreciate that, and we also appreciate that Mr. Fahge met with Daniel before he returned to school. But it's clear to us some of the evidences you used to accuse Daniel was spread inside the school." My mom said.

"The students just need to learn how to treat each other, be nice not mean to other people. We try to create a no hate community at school." Mrs. Bush continued. It seemed to calm everybody down.

"We also want to put this behind us as soon as possible. So send your statement as soon as you can, and I promise I will review immediately. But next week is spring break, so I am not sure how quick we can move this forward." Mr. Fahge said.

"It won't take long for Daniel to finalize the statement, but I am not sure whether he would be able to send it to you this week. You have a biology test tomorrow, right?" My dad said.

"Yeah, I have a biology test tomorrow." I answered.

"Well, send in whenever you can, and we will go from there." Mr. Fahge said.

The terrible meeting ended like that and I returned to my class. Why were they so reluctant to help me?

FROM THE TERRIBLE meeting we sensed we needed to be prepared to have a long battle with the school and we might not be able to solve this issue within the school. So we forwarded my statement to Mr. Ralph for review. By Friday, Mr. Ralph returned the statement with an email to my parents:

Dear Michael and Anna,

I have attached a cleanup copy of Daniel's statement. I reorganized it a bit and fixed a little English. I tried to leave it in his own words as much as possible. If it is ok with you, thenyou can send it to Mr. Fahge with a note asking him to consider removing the suspension from Daniel's record. You should ask for clarification as to why Daniel was suspended.

As I go back through all the emails from the school, it is clear that Daniel is not really being suspended for much of anything to do with Fred Guo's phone. The school obviously thinks that Daniel had been saying bad things about other students on-line are what they call "cyber-bullying". The school does not follow a definition of "cyber-bullying" that is consistent with state law. I believe that schools are very concerned about any comments they think are "anti-gay" or "homophobic." I think this is the real reason Daniel was suspended. It is unfortunate that the school will not give you all the supposed evidence they have against Daniel.

At this point, I seriously doubt that Mr. Fahge will change the decision. What other kids are doing does not matter to him. They probably want to make an example of Daniel. You will need to consider if you will want to appeal to the Superintendent.

Let me know if you have more questions or need more help.

Ralph

The assessment from Mr. Ralph is not very encouraging. It seems if the school was determined to punish me, or they had to stick to their original decision to prevent from being accused of wrongdoing. Their focus or concerns were no justice or what if right but protecting themselves. Unfortunately, there is not much I could do about it. It does not make sense to me why a student as a minor could not enjoy the constitutional right.

Chapter Twelve

SPRING BREAK

I was really thankful that Spring Break was coming. So I just went through the motions of school that week. However, it was a terrible time to have my mind taken off of school work. The AP class teachers were beginning to prepare us for the fast-approaching AP Tests, other teachers maybe saw that they were running out of time to cover all the necessary material. It was mentally and emotionally draining. Any physical energy I had was probably diminished as well.

In the beginning of the process, I was so eager to fight for myself and thought that it would not affect me at all. I was wrong.

It wasn't that I always thought about it. It was the constant attention I was forced to pay to it. Some days, I might be doing my homework upstairs, without a single brain cell focused on the suspension situation. But my parents would be downstairs in the study figuring out new ways to appeal the decision. If I went downstairs to get a drink of water I would see both of their slippers at the doorway of the study and know that both of them were in there discussing my situation.

It was even worse when I had to go into that study and tell them details about what happened so they didn't make a mistake.

After a trip downstairs like that, it would take me sometimes fifteen minutes to get refocused on what I had previously been doing. Since I had never gone through the loss of life of someone close to me or any rifts in my immediate family, it was probably the most stressful time of my life. But I tried to hide it as best I could.

On the Tuesday of my spring break, I was going to go meet with a lawyer. My dad had located a law firm in North Hills, which was about a forty minute drive that specialized in education law.

They granted one free meeting with one of their lawyers.

The appointment with the lawyer was scheduled for 10:30am. My dad went to work and came to pick me up around 9:45am.

At that point, I was a little embarrassed to see a lawyer. I always thought of lawyers as people who were like the ones in John Grisham's books who defended murderers and tax evaders. Facebook crime? A few dirty words? I didn't think that it was appropriate to see a lawyer over.

It was a rainy Tuesday. My dad drove on the 90% empty highway with me in the front passenger's seat. We were going to make it to their offices with time to spare.

However, the road we were traveling on was closed down for repairs. Everybody had to turn back and go a different route. Great, we had just wasted twenty five minutes because the other route to North Hills required us to go back the way we came. And then go a different route.

We arrived at the law firm about forty minutes late. As I said, I was a little bit ashamed to see the lawyer. The law firm was located in a suite in a medium sized office building. There was a very old elevator that took us to the second story of the building. It took a while, but we found the door that led to their suite. Just by the looks of it so far, it didn't seem to be a very large or established law firm.

We were met at the front desk by a very nice lady that had us fill out a clipboard. As my dad filled out the information, I looked around their office. The ground was covered by a deep emerald carpet. The furniture was all rather antique even if not of the top quality. There was a corner that was designated for a copying machine. There were also a few large book shelves and a huge file cabinet that seemed to have a million sheets of paper in it.

The lawyer we were meeting with was named Samantha Johnson. She looked no more than twenty five years old but talked like someone who was fifty.

"So what can I help you with?"

"He got in trouble at school for cyberbullying and we don't think that the punishment handed down toward him is entirely fair," my dad said.

I just sat there twiddling my thumbs.

"Okay, what kind of situation are we dealing with right now?" she asked.

"We are trying to appeal the decision of the school but so far we are not getting very far," my dad said.

"Yes, that is often the case when students take on the school system," she said, "there are new laws that protect the schools a lot and make it very difficult for anyone to win a decision against a school."

"Okay," my dad said.

"Anyways, please tell me more because I can't really help you until you tell me more about the situation," she said.

"He got hit by another at school and didn't hit back. Afterwards he told the principal as he was told. And then one day later, he was told that he was suspended for two days for cyberbullying. He says that some of the evidence that was used against him was altered to make him look guilty," my dad said.

"Okay," she said.

"The evidence the school provided to us to support the suspension is not very convincing. All of them were collected online. But the school did not show us all evidence because they claim that the evidence that they have of Daniel bullying other students is through interviews they did with other students" my dad said as he handed a few printouts to the lawyer.

She spent a couple of minutes to read the evidence school provided. "Among the three pieces only this Facebook discussion on March 31st seems directly related to the incident on April 1st. The other Facebook discussion of the tennis team is more than 1 year old, and trying to link a Twitter input 9 months ago to what happen on April 1st is really a stretch."

"That what we thought" said my dad.

"The discussion on March 31st is about Fred Guo," she said.

"Yes, that is the boy who hit him," my dad answered.

"Okay, so did he post this first? Did Fred see this post and get angry?" she asked.

"No, my son, Daniel, says that he posted this after Fred made a phone call to him and said things that angered him," my dad said.

"Okay, then if this is all true, I don't really see any cyberbullying taking place," the lawyer said.

"But, the assistant principal says that the comments made on that status by Daniel regarding Fred are threats against Fred," my dad said.

"I don't really see a threat, oh, 'I'll guarantee him the second swing'? In legal terms, it would be very difficult to prove that as a threat. Beside some very bad language, which let's face it is not that uncommon these days among teenagers, I really don't see that much that could get your son suspended."

There was a brief period of silence. The three of us just exchanged glances back and forth toward each other.

"I want to ask how he feels about it," she said.

"Well, I know I have faults in this situation. And I've learned a lot from this but I just feel that they punished me harsher than I deserve and that I've been accused of doing things that I didn't do," I said.

"So you feel wronged," she commented.

"I feel like the decision they made might have been a little bit subjective and pretty unfair. And I've lost a lot of trust in the school system," I said.

"Okay," she said, "Do you feel like they rushed to a conclusion?"

"Well, I just think some of the claims they made against me were not proven yet. I don't think they've proved what they are saying I did. And that they are overlooking a lot of what other people did to cause me to do certain things," I said.

"So you're saying all these negative actions you have committed are reactionary," she said.

"Yes, and I also feel that instead of being innocent until they prove me guilty, that I'm guilty and that I have to go through all of this to prove myself innocent," I said, "And the way they handled this situation also bothers me. There really seems to be some favoritism involved," I said.

"Do you have any evidence to support your claim the favoritism was involved?" she asked.

"Fred's father used to be a teacher at school." I answered.

"OK, then certainly you can make the favoritism argument." She said.

"The school claims that they had more evidence but would not share with us. How are we going to appeal the suspension without seeing all the evidence?" My dad asked.

"This is pretty common. The school has to protect confidential information. However, parents have absolute right to gain access to student's record at school. The suspension will be part of student record, and as a result, anything used to support the suspension decision should be considered as part of student's record. So the parents have the right to access them, but you have to submit the request in writing." She explained.

"What is your overall comment on this case based what you had seen?" My dad asked.

"Overall I believe the school did a very poor job of handling this. First of all, for the official suspension notice, they checked a wrong box. If the offense is cyberbullying, they should check (i) instead of (d). Secondly, the evidence they provided is not very strong to support the allegation." She said.

"Does that mean that we would have a good chance to overturn the suspension?" My dad asked.

"Not necessary. First, you don't know what other evidence the school has. Secondly, school has a lot levy to punish cyberbullying. In recent years cyberbullying has become a hot issue and it does not take much to be accused of cyberbullying. All needed is somebody claimed to be hurt by what you said online. So the best way to avoid the trouble is not saying anything stupid online. More importantly, if you want to overturn the suspension, you have to go through the appeal process with school and the school district. So at the end of the day it all depends how school want to handle it." She said.

It sounds to me that school can do whatever it wants and there is little we could do about it. I thought.

"What is the procedure of appeal? We asked the principal but it seems they do not have a formal appeal procedure." My dad asked.

"For suspension, the California Education Code did not specify the extract appeal procedure, and leave that to education board or school district to define. But in general you first appeal to the principal, then the superintendent of the school district." She answered.

"What's next?" My dad asked.

"If you don't agree with the decision made by the superintendent, you then appeal to the education board, and then the next step is to appeal to county education board. That's pretty much the end of it." She answered.

"Could we go to the court?" My dad asked.

"Yes, you can. But the court may not take on the case. A lot of judge tends to believe that it is better to leave education matters to the educators, and therefore are very reluctant to weigh in on education issues." She said.

"So it's pretty hard to suit the school in Education law." My dad said.

"That in general is true." She said.

"How about bring a lawsuit outside education law?" my dad asked.

"To make a civil lawsuit, you have to be in a protected status. But it seems both Fred Guo and Harrison Oh are Asian Americans, so you cannot claim discrimination." She said.

So I would have a better chance to prove my innocent if Fred was a Caucasian or even black? That sounds ridicules.

"So it seems we do not have a clear path." My dad commented.

"Well, for suspension the appeal process is not clearly defined in the education code. We certainly can help you to go through the appeal process. But quite frankly, most of our clients are fighting expulsion. For expulsion the law has specific requirements that the school must follow. For suspension, not a lot of students or parents really want to fight the school, maybe just because it's not worth the time and efforts." She seems very honest. Although I was impressed that she gave us honest opinion, and did not simple trying the get a business, the lack of enthusiasm from her part suggested it is going to be hard to overturn the suspension.

"What would be you assessment of the probability of success if appeal?" My dad asked a specific question.

"I would say 50-50. The evidence I had seen dose not really support the accusation. But on the other hand, if the school insist, it is hard to overturn the suspension." She answered.

It sounds like even the school did not have very strong evidence against me, it is still very hard to prove my innocent. Something of the education system must be wrong. It seems to me that the education code was written to protect the school, not the student.

"May I ask your charge rate?" My dad asked.

"Our charge rate is $310/h. If you decided to use our service, you would have to pay upfront $1500 retainer fee after signing the agreement, and that will give you 5 hours of service. After that we charge hour by hour." She answered.

"How much work will it be?" My dad asked.

"I think the first 5 hours should be able to cover all the work up to appeal to the superintendent." She answered.

"How about if we want to go to the court?"

"That will be a lot more. It will cost maybe $25,000 just to prepare court paper." She answered.

"But if the judge decides to not take up the case then that $25000 would be wasted." My dad said.

"That's true." She answered. "You need make decision what you would want to do. I will be more than happy to provide the service. Here is my card. You can either email me or call me when you need our service."

"Thank you."

To be honest, the meeting was pretty boring. Samantha Johnson was incredibly attentive when she listened to the case my dad and I were making to her but it didn't really seem like she was in any way feeling the same sense of wrongdoing on the school's part that I did. At least she was honest with us, but she wasn't too optimistic about our chances to get my suspension appealed.

Chapter Thirteen

BECAUSE I WAS having some trouble dealing with all the stress that came with appealing the suspension, my dad looked up a psychiatrist for me. He found one that had his office near our house and was covered by our insurance plan.

I must admit that I was a little bit reluctant to see a psychiatrist. I always envisioned suicidal people or just people with extreme emotional problems as the only ones to see psychiatrists. Maybe I was a little stressed out, but I felt mentally stable.

My psychiatrist's name is John Glenn. From the looks of it, he did not work for any larger corporation. His office was in a building that housed many other small businesses. The setup of his office surprised me but maybe I didn't really know what to expect.

For the very first appointment, I agreed to have my dad join me to discuss the problems I was going through since the incident at school happened.

As I walked into John's office, I noticed that there weren't any file cabinets with locks on them or anything abnormal. In fact, his office looked more like a normal study room of someone's house. There was a desk with a phone on it. There was a rocking chair where John would sit and a couch where my dad and I would sit. There was a small coffee table with a box of Kleenex on it and a bookshelf with many books that included *Chicken Soup for the Soul* and other similar books.

John himself was a very tall and lanky man. He was probably in his mid forties and looked like an incredibly pleasant fellow.

"Hi, my name is Michael, this is my son Daniel," my dad said with a smile as he shook hands with John.

"Hello Michael, nice to meet you. Hi Daniel?" John asked.

"Yeah, Daniel," I said quietly extending my hand to receive a handshake.

"Please, have a seat," he said.

During the car ride to the psychiatrist's office, I tried to think about what would be appropriate to say and what I wanted to focus on during the time we would be talking. I thought of a few things to say, but still was hoping that John would take control and ask me questions which would make it much easier for me.

Instead, he seemed to want to do most of the listening and asked me what he could do to help.

"So Daniel, and Michael, what can I do to help you, what kind of assistance would you like from me?" he asked.

My dad motioned for me to answer the question so I said, "Well I've been dealing with a pretty tough situation that I've never experienced before and just felt that seeing a psychiatrist would help take my mind off these things."

"Of course, but how would you like our sessions to go. Some of my patients do all of the talking when they come and just sort of vent their emotions, and that's totally fine. Others maybe just ask me questions and ask for my advice on how to handle certain situations. I'm perfectly fine and okay with either form," he said in a quiet but firm tone.

"Probably a mixture of the two, I feel like I really want to know how to deal with different personalities better. How to refrain myself and stop myself from getting into these types of situations again and how to just keep my emotions in check or use my emotions positively," I said.

"Okay," said John.

The meeting went well, my dad did most of the talking while describing the actual facts of the situation I was in while I talked about how it affected me. We agreed on a time to meet again and also agreed that next time I would talk to John alone in hopes that I would open up more.

After that first meeting, I began to meet with John by myself. At first, it felt a little bit weird talking to him about all of the issues I had at school because a lot of it was explaining the situation to him. But after awhile, I became more comfortable with John and our conversations flowed better. We touched on subjects ranging from learning to drive to school matters.

I had questions going into these sessions with John because I didn't know what an appointment with a psychologist entailed. But after months of seeing John every other week, I really began to enjoy the sessions. It was just a place to talk to someone who was neutral on the subjects. He wouldn't ever tell me I was right or I was wrong but he would challenge me to think about why I felt a certain way and question why I really was motivated to do a certain thing. I matured a lot and learned to balance my emotion with some logic.

I decided that when I grew up I would continue to see a psychologist on a bi-weekly basis if I could afford the time and money to see one.

Chapter Fourteen

THE SPRING BREAK quickly came to an end. We decided to send my statement on Saturday evening. I had the statement ready last Friday but we decided not sending it until Saturday since the principal won't be able to review it during spring break and we did not want it lost during the week.

April 16, 2010
To: Mr. Fahge,

From: Daniel Liu,

These are the facts of what happened to me and why my suspension was wrong.

1. *I was assaulted by Fred Guo on Thursday, April 1, 2010. The following are the specific actions by Fred Guo:*

   a. *Fred Guo first threatened me over the phone on Wednesday afternoon. He used Josh Hsu's phone. I told him I did not take or have his phone.*

b. *On Thursday, Fred threatened me by asking if I wanted to fight him. He then faked a punch to my face that made me flinch, so I stood up in case he was going to hit me.*

c. *He looked around and then said, "There are no cameras around here so I could bitch-slap you across the face and nobody would know. Did you know that? What would you do if I just bitch-slapped you across the face right now?"*

d. *Fred hit me in the back of the head near my left ear.*

Evidence/Witness: Picture taken by Mrs. Bush, Robert Sampson, Nathan Cho, George Tang

2. *I never stole Fred's cell phone or headphones. George Tang and David Lee can prove it. After I told Fred I did not take him phone on Wednesday afternoon he never called me again. On Thursday, he went directly to George to claim his headphones. This also proves that Fred knew that George took his phone and headphones. Using a joke I made on Twitter 9 months ago as evidence to accuse me of theft is wrong.*

3. *I did not bully Fred Guo.*

a. *What was written on my status was an angry response to a phone call he made to me in which he threatened me. I told Mrs. Bush about this phone call on Thursday when I reported that Fred assaulted me. To prove it, I told her that Fred had borrowed Josh Hsu's phone and told her how to spell Hsu. However, During Friday's conversation with Mrs. Bush, I never heard anything mentioned about the phone call. Mr.*

> *Fahge claims that he had never heard anything about that phone call until my parents met with him on Monday.*

b. *I did not make any threats toward Fred with my status.*

c. *The Facebook dialog between me and George on Wednesday evening was about the threats Fred made toward to both me and George.*

d. *I have not had Fred added as a "friend" on Facebook for about a year. Therefore he cannot see my status. If I wanted to bully Fred Guo I would not post on my status since it would not serve the purpose.*

e. *The other picture (Tennis team) was more than a year ago, and the comment I made than was just a joke. It also is not cyber-bullying, and there is no connection between that picture and the incident on Thursday April 1st.*

4. *The accusation of my "behavior leading to a fight" is not true.*

a. *"Physical altercation" is not a correct description of the incident happened on April 1st. The truth is that Fred Guo assaulted me, and I never fought back. How come that was considered to be a "physical altercation"?*

b. *I did not provoke the assault. The evidences provided above demonstrated that (1) I did not take Fred's phone or headphone and (2) I did not bully Fred Guo.*

c. *In fact, for the whole process I had been exercise self control to prevent escalating.*

d. *When Fred Guo wrongfully accused me of taking his phone and threatened me over the phone on March 31, I did not say anything malicious back to him.*

e. *On Thursday, April 1ˢᵗ, Fred Guo repeatedly threatened me, but I never threatened back or accepted his challenge to fight him.*

f. *Even after he hit me on my head, I did not fight back.*

g. *I reported the incident to school authority to deescalate the situation.*

5. *I did not bully Harrison.*

    a. *On Friday Mrs. Bush showed me a Facebook printout but would not allow me to have a close look. I believe the printout is an online conversation that I had with Harrison Oh from about a month ago but was altered. In reality, Harrison started the conversation and insulted/ threatened me first.*

    b. *Those online conversations happened outside school during after school hours, and had nothing to do with school activities. These posts were never mentioned during school between Harrison and me*

    c. *In addition, the subject had nothing to do with Fred and his phone. What does Harrison have to do with my suspension?*

6. *School authorities are using evidence against me that has nothing to do with me being assaulted by Fred or Fred's phone/headphone being taken.*

a. *Ms. Bush said she had a printout from urbandictionary.com and that I said something bad about James Bake. I have nothing to do with urbandictionary.com. James Bake has nothing to do with Fred or his phone. I was not provided a copy of this document. What does James Bake have to do with my suspension?*

b. *Printout of an online conversation that I had with Harrison Oh from about a month ago. I had reason to believe that the evidence was tampered with but Mrs. Bush would not let me to have a copy of this paper.*

c. *A Facebook picture of the tennis team from a year ago that has nothing to do with Fred's phone. The talk by the team was joking stuff.*

d. *A twitter printout that is a joke I made on Twitter 9 months ago and was used as evidence to accuse me of theft. Does the school truly believe that I planned to steal the headphones nine months ahead of time?*

I would like to have a copy of these first two pieces of paper.

7. *I was unfairly treated.*

a. *The whole process started with a conflict between George Tang and Fred Guo over Fred's phone being taken and ended up with me being assaulted by Fred Guo. During this process, I did not take Fred Guo's phone or headphones. I was a victim of an assault by Fred Guo and reported the incident to school authorities. I was then was punished with suspension. If I did not report the incident nothing would have* happened. However, after I reported incident, I was punished more than the people who physically assaulted me.

b. The decision to suspend me was made without giving me a chance to defend myself.

c. After I reported the incident on Thursday and before my suspension decision was made on Friday, school authorities prepared new allegations and gathered evidence against me but never interviewed me and would not show me all the evidence.

d. It was claimed that I was given opportunity to defend myself on Friday when Ms. Bush informed me the suspension. However, Ms. Bush started the conversation by showing some of the evidences against me and then telling me that the decision was already made. Based on an email by Mr. Fahge on April 5, Mrs. Bush accused me of being "very defensive" during that meeting, indicating that the purpose of that meeting was not for me to defend myself

e. It was also claimed that my conversation with Mr. Fahge after school on Friday was another chance for me to make my argument. In fact, I specifically asked him, "Is there anything I can do right now?" and I was told I could only appeal after the fact, which indicates that this is not an opportunity for me to defend myself since the decision was made.

8. I am not a bully and have not been doing any cyber-bullying. If I am, then most of the students at CHS are guilty also. I can print out many similar

> *pages from many students. I do not remember that CHS has ever provided meaningful training about cyber-bullying and in the student handbook there is no definition on what constitutes cyber-bullying or a guideline for disciplinary action. I do not understand what this has to do with Fred hitting me and my unfair suspension.*

We scan the statement into a pdf file, and my parent drafted an email to Mr. Fahge:

Dear Mr. Fahge,

It was unfortunate that the meeting on Thursday (4/8/2010) morning did not produce meaningful results. It is obvious we had different understanding of "give" or "giving" you used in your email below. As non-native English speakers, we are especially vulnerable to such misunderstanding.

Attached is Daniel's statement per your request. Please review it and let us know if you have any questions or would like to schedule another meeting. We hope you, as a neutral judge for due process, would carefully examine all the evidences including Daniel's statement to reach a fair, just and unbiased conclusion.

As mentioned before, we would like to satisfactorily resolve this matter by removing the suspension from Daniel's school record. In case you still do not agree, we would like to receive the following documents so that we can better prepare our appeal to the Superintendent:

> 1. *All the evidences school gathered. So far we were provided with only three pieces of evidences. Since the suspension would become official record for Daniel,*

we have the right to have not only the suspension notice but also all the supporting documents.

2. *Copies of any rules that you based on to reach the suspension decision.*

Thank you for spending time reviewing this issue. We certainly hope that this matter could be satisfactorily resolved without additional appeals.

Sincerely yours,
Michael Liu
Anna Liu

AFTER SENDING OUT the statement, I knew I could be called into the principal's office at any moment.

We did not received anything from the principal on Monday, and my dad said we would give him 48 hours before sending follow up email with him. By Tuesday morning my parents received an email from Mr. Fahge:

April 20ʰ, 2010

Dear Mr. and Mrs. Liu,

Hello. I just wanted to let you know that I received Daniel's letter and am currently reviewing it and examining the evidence. I will get back to you tomorrow with my findings.

Sincerely,

Andrew Fahge

Principal
Chester High School

So it seemed like we would get the results from him by Wednesday.

But nothing happened on Wednesday. I was very anxious, but my parents did not follow up with the principal immediately since if the principal sent his decision through mail it might take a day or two to reach us. But by Friday evening it was clear we would not receive anything, and my parents decided to send the following email:

April 23rd, 2010

Dear Mr. Fahge,

We have not received any notice (email or regular mail) from you regarding your review on Daniel's suspension. We can understand that you may have to delay your decision for various reasons, and the purpose of this email is just to make sure that the communication is not lost.

Thank you and regards,

Sincerely,

Michael Liu
Anna Liu

This time, the principal replied immediately.

Very busy days, I am still reviewing the case. I will complete my review early next week.

Sincerely,

Andrew Fahge
Principal
Chester High School

Why did it take so long for him to review the case and make a decision? Last time it took him less than three hours to send out the email claiming to have significant evidence against me, but now more than a week had come and past and he still could not put together a response? Well, this may be a good sign, at least we got his attention, and hopefully he is willing to spend a little more time on it.

He was not in a good position. If he did not remove the suspension, we had made it clear we would appeal to the superintendent, which would expose all the wrongdoing to the superintendent. If he agreed with our request and remove the suspension, he'd worry that we may demand a formal apology and that would put the school and Mrs. Bush in a liable legal position. We clearly stated that all we wanted is to remove the suspension, but he had a reason to be worried.

Chapter Fifteen

NOTHING HAPPENED ON Monday and Tuesday, but on Wednesday, I was called into principal's office once again during the middle of Spanish class. This was an opportunity given to me to make my point, but it was impossible for me to do so. He wasn't listening. When he did, he was listening while thinking about how to shoot down my argument. He really just gave off the sense that he wasn't trying to help me that he was against me. Mrs. Bush was against me. The whole school did not want to believe my side of the story. But they were so eager to believe everything Fred said and everything Harrison said. I wasn't bullying Fred or Harrison. Harrison or Fred weren't bullying me. The school was bullying me. I was playing the piano for a cow.

But near the end of the meeting, he proposed something that made me think.

"So, after all that's been said, I am agreeing to cut your suspension down to one day instead of the original two days," he said.

"Thank you," I said without really meaning it.

"I hope that now we can just let it go. If I cut it down to one day will you just let it all go because it's a huge burden on all of us that we don't want," he said.

Why was he trying to force me to let it go? I wasn't going to let it go, but I just agreed half-heartedly.

At the end of the meeting Mr. Fahge told me that the system in place wasn't perfect and that I had to learn to navigate it.

Generally, that's good advice. But for me, navigating the system would be like trying to navigate a car in the opposite lane of the highway. Everything was coming at me, trying to destroy me. It was impossible.

I told my parents about the meeting, but we were still waiting for the formal notice from the principal. It is not clear why he did not immediately contact my parents until Friday:

April 30th, 2010

Thank you for your patience.

Upon review of Daniel's letter and all of the evidence collected, I have decided to affirm Ms. Bush's decision to suspend Daniel but to reduce it to one day. Daniel and I discussed the reasons for this and while he may not have been in agreement, I think he understood the rationale.

I will notify all of his teachers to allow him to make up any work missed on the second day of suspension.

I advised Daniel to learn from this experience, to understand how the system works, not to reject it, rather to figure out how to navigate it. One of the most critical lessons is to be extremely careful about what he puts in writing, whether it's on paper or electronic. We discussed what is incontrovertible evidence as opposed to hearsay (such as what is reported to have been said on the phone).

I hope we can put this all behind us. Of course, if you are opposed to my decision, then you may appeal to the Superintendent.

Sincerely,

Andrew Fahge
Principal
Chester High School

That is what he comes up with after two weeks of review. He did not respond to any question I asked and did not give any reason to justify the suspension. It seems to me he is simply trying to protect Mrs. Bush for all the mistakes she made. Also he totally ignored our request for evidence.

SINCE WE WERE not satisfied with the decision and the principal totally ignored our request for evidence, my parents immediately email the principal to let him know that we would appeal to the superintendent and asked again for the evidence:

April 30th, 2010
Dear Mr. Fahge,

Thank you for your time and effort to review this case. We also hope that we can put this all behind us, but unfortunately we still cannot understand the rational of your decision. Therefore, we have to appeal this case to the Superintendent.

Please provide the following documents at your earliest convenience:

1. *All the pieces of evidence you have. So far we have been provided with only three copies as evidence. We need to have all the evidence you gathered.*
2. *Copies of any rules that you based your suspension decision on. If a formal written request is required to obtain the above documents, please let us know. In case you can not provide, please inform us and also let us know the reason for not providing the above documents.*

Thanks and looking forward to hearing from you soon.

Sincerely,

Michael Liu and Anna Liu

And all received was a one line response without a salutation. It was curt, stand-offish, but direct.

At this point, all of your communications need to be directed to the Superintendent.

Ted Fahge

Principal
Chester High School

It is clear now the he was determined to avoid any direct discussion with us. So we had no choice but to appeal to the superintendent.

Chapter Sixteen

THE FIRST STEP is to ask for evidence. So my parent sent a formal letter to the superintendent:

MICHAEL LIU AND ANNA LIU
1900 Pleasant Hill Drive
Richland, CA 93653

May 3rd, 2010

Megan Anderson,
Superintendent
Chester Unified School District
3231 Euclid Avenue
Chester, CA 93435

Re: Request for record related to Suspension—Daniel Liu

Dear Superintendent,

We are writing to request for information related to suspension imposed to our son, Daniel Liu, a junior at

Chester High School, on April 2nd, 2010. This request is made pursuant to Cal. Educ. Code Section 49070 and any and all applicable School District Procedures and Policies.

Specifically, please provide the following documents at your earliest convenience:

1. *Copies of all the records related to the suspension including all the evidences school collected.*
2. *Copies of school/district rules/policies that the school based on to reach the suspension decision.*
3. *Copies of procedure for appeal of the suspension.*

We believe we have a right to access the records and such access is a critical first step to understand why the suspension was imposed.

We look forward to hearing from you. We can be reached by phone at 413-228-3859 (cell) or 413-765-8978 (home) or email at mliu2100@hotmail.com.

Very truly yours,

Michael Liu
Anna Liu

First the superintendent responded quickly, and in a very formal format:

Chester Unified School District
3231 Euclid Avenue
Chester, CA 93435

May 4th, 2010

Chumeng Li

MICHAEL LIU AND ANNA LIU
1900 Pleasant Hill Drive
Richland, CA 93653

Re: Request for record related to Suspension—Daniel Liu

Dear Parents:

This is in response to your letter to me dated May 3, 2010. In your letter, you requested that the District provide records related to the suspension of your son, Daniel Liu—a junior at Chester High School, on April 2, 2010. The following documents were requested:

1. *Copies of all the records related to the suspension including all evidence that the school collected.*
2. *Copies of school/district rules/policies that the school based to reach the suspension decision.*
3. *Copies of the procedure to appeal a suspension.*

In an effort to satisfy your request, I am gathering said documents and will have information relating to your request within 10 (ten) business days.

If you have any further questions, please call me at (413) 855-6673.

Sincerely,

Megan Anderson
Superintendent

We considered this is a good sign, at least she took this issue seriously.

But unfortunately, she did not keep her promise. Nothing happened after 10 business days. After 12 business days, my parents sent a follow up email to her:

May 20ᵗʰ, 2010

Dear Superintendent,
We have not received the documents we requested in our letter to you on May 3rd, 2010. We will appreciate if you could send the documents to us at your earliest convenience.

Thank you and regards,
Sincerely,

Michael Liu and Anna Liu

Still no response, so two days' later they had to send another email to ask:

May 24ᵗʰ 2010

Dear Superintendent,
We are still waiting for the documents we requested on May 3rd, 2010. We will appreciate if you could give us an update. Thanks and regards,
Michael Liu and Anna Liu

This time we received a one line email from the superintendent on Monday evening:

Hi,

They will be sent to you tomorrow.
Megan Anderson

Superintendent
Chester Unified School District

WE RECEIVED THE mail two days later.

Chester Unified School District
3231 Euclid Avenue
Chester, CA 93435

May 24, 2010

Michael Liu and Anna Liu
1900 Pleasant Hill Drive
Richland, CA 93653

Re: Request for record related to Suspension—Daniel Liu

Dear Parents:

Enclosed please find the following:

a. *A copy of the record relating to the suspension of Danial Liu dated 4/2/20100*
b. *Evidence related to the suspension*

c. *Board policy used in the suspension decision: Please refer to AR 5144.1(e) #22—Engaged in an act of bullying, and AR 5144.l(c) # 11 Disrupted school activities.*

You may not appeal the suspension decision; however you may challenge the student record. Please refer to AR 5125.3(a-b).

Sincerely,

Megan Anderson
Superintendent

Enclosures:
Exhibit 1 Suspension
Exhibit 2 Discipline Report
Exhibit 3 Evidence to support suspension
Exhibit 4 Board Policy and AR—Discipline
Exhibit 5 Board Policy and AR—Student records

We were shocked that that the superintendent said that we could not appeal. The principal told us more than one times that we could appeal to the superintendent, but now she said we could not. We asked and never received a formal procedure for appeal, and now it seems they just want to play the game. Since there is no written procedure from the school district, so they can do whatever they want. Is it that convenient for them?

If she insists the we could not appeal, she would have to admit that what Mr. Fahge told us was wrong, then we would argue that the suspension decision was made and reviewed by someone who is not competent since he did not even know what the procedure is. So the school district must reevaluate the suspension.

My parent sent another letter to the superintendent.

__MICHAEL LIU AND ANNA LIU__
__1900 Pleasant Hill Drive__
__Richland, CA 93653__

May 25ᵗʰ, 2010

Megan Anderson, Superintendent
Chester Unified School District
3231 Euclid Avenue
Chester, CA 93435

Dear Superintendent,

Thanks for preparing and sending us the documents related to Daniel's suspension.

1. *We would like to seek clarification on your statement that we "may not appeal the suspension decision".*
   a. *Mr. Fahge informed us that we might appeal to you if we did not agree with school's decision. Here we attached two emails (on April 6ᵗʰ, 2010 and and April 30ᵗʰ, 2010) from Mr. Fahge.*
   b. *Should we consider this statement as your response to our request of "Copies of procedure for appeal of the suspension"?*
2. *Please clarify whether the document you sent us contains ALL the evidences used to reach the suspension decision.*

3. *We believe that the suspension decision was unreasonable, unfair, not supported by facts or evidences, and not consistent with California Education Codes or school district policies. The decision making process was at least unprofessional. If we could not appeal, is there any other alternative to address our concerns?*

We hope you would understand that our primary concern is a safe and welcoming learning environment and equal educational opportunity for Daniel and all students at the school. This incident had profound impact on Daniel, and our only goal is to eventually make this incident a positive learning experience for Daniel so that he can believe in the fundamental ideas of fairness, due process and equal justice in this land. We will do our best to help him, and certainly hope we could receive helps from you. Therefore, we will appreciate very much you could respond at your earliest convenience and provide specific guidance so that we could satisfactorily solve this matter soon.

Thanks and with regards,

Sincerely,
Michael Liu and Anna Liu

This time, she did not even wait for the hard copy to be mailed to her, she replied immediately:

Chumeng Li

May 25th, 2010

Dear Mr. and Mrs. Liu,

I am considering your letter a challenge to the suspension of your son. I will conduct an investigation and you will be notified by mail of my decision.

Cordially,
Megan Anderson

Superintendent
Chester Unified School District

The prompt and direct response was appreciated and she seemed to be willing to be fair. My parents immediately responded.

May 25th, 2010

Dear Superintendent,

Thank you for agreeing to investigate the suspension of our son Daniel Liu.

We will prepare and send you a document summarizing the facts and evidence we have.

Thanks again and best regards,

Michael Liu and Anna Liu

MY PARENTS THEN read through numerous emails, researched many state education codes and laws to come up with points where the school administrators either missed or did not follow correctly. Not only were there problems with what they accused me of doing, more alarmingly, there were problems with the process they took to reach the conclusion of suspending me.

MICHAEL LIU AND ANNA LIU
1900 Pleasant Hill Drive
Richland, CA 93653

June 1ˢᵗ, 2010

Megan Anderson,
Superintendent
Chester Unified School District
3231 Euclid Avenue
Chester, CA 93435

Dear Superintendent,
Thank you for investigating the recent suspension of our son Daniel Liu. We are writing to request removal of the suspension from Daniel's school record.

1. ***The suspension decision is not supported by facts or evidence***
   Based on the Official Notice of Suspension, the Cause for Suspension is "disrupt school activity or defy school authority (48900(k))" and the offense time was 1:15 pm, 4/1/10. Astonishingly, among all the documents the school provided, there is not one iota of evidence to show what happened at that time.

During lunch time on April 1st, 2010, Daniel was physically assaulted by another student on school ground. He did not fight back and reported the assault to the school authorities. In no way did his behavior "Disrupt school activities" nor did he defy "valid authority." Therefore the reason for the suspension of Daniel was fundamentally wrong.

Two specific actions identified on the suspension notice were also not supported by facts or evidence.

First of all, there was never a fight. What happened on April 1st, 2010 was that Daniel was physically assaulted but never fought back. Therefore, "behavior leading to a fight" is a false statement.

We noticed that the title of Exhibit 3 in the document you sent to us is "Facebook Screenshot", which reflects the fact that the school exclusively used web-based information to make accusation against Daniel. Almost all pieces of evidence were online activities that happened long time ago, outside school, not during school hour, never had any impact on school activities, and has nothing to do with what happened on April 1st, 2010. The interpretation of those web based information are highly subjective and disputable, and in school policy there is no clear definition of cyber bullying or guideline on what the disciplinary action should be. The school's justification of its decision to suspend Daniel with such evidences is fundamentally a misapplication of California law and school policy.

More importantly, as we will describe below, majority of the evidence not only did not support the accusation against Daniel but also raised questions about practices and conducts demonstrated during the investigation and decision making process.

(1) *Comments on tennis team picture (Page 9 in the document you sent to us on May 24th, 2010)*
   (a) *There is no connection between those comments and the physical assault on Thursday April 1st, 2010. It is a leap of illogic to use a harmless joke made on March 24, 2009 as an excuse of physical assault committed on April 1st, 2010.*
   (b) *It is obvious that those students were trading jokes. If the school really wants to pass judgment on those comments, how can you argue both that gay, like others, must be protected from discriminations and that "gay" is an offensive word? Will school consider the comment by Omar Khaled an insult to George Tang and comment by George Tang an insult to Nathan Cho?*

(2) *Online dialogue between Daniel and George Tang on the evening of March 31, 2010 (Page 8)*
   a) *It was written on Daniel's Facebook status which was in private setting. School did not have the right to access it. Unless the school can prove that they obtained this evidence legally, it must not be used as evidence at all.*
   b) *This dialogue was a discussion about the threats Fred Guo made toward to both Daniel and George Tang, and was triggered by a phone call by Fred Guo at 5:00 pm this day when*

> *he wrongfully accused Daniel and made the threat. Therefore it is not an evidence to prove that Daniel's action lead to a fight.*
>
> c) *As pointed above, Daniel's Facebook status was in private setting. Fred Guo was not a Facebook "friend" of Daniel and could not see Daniel's Facebook status. Therefore this conversation cannot be a cause for the physically assault committed by Fred Guo.*
>
> d) *The only linkage between this online conversation and what actually happened on April 1ˢᵗ, 2010 is that Fred Guo made the threat and then implemented.*

In fact, for the whole process Daniel had been exercising self control. When Fred Guo wrongfully accused Daniel of taking his phone and threatened him over the phone on March 31ˢᵗ 2010, Daniel did not say anything malicious back to him. On Thursday, April 1ˢᵗ 2010, Fred Guo repeatedly threatened Daniel, but Daniel never threatened back or accepted his challenge to fight him. Even after he hit Daniel's head, Daniel did not fight back, and reported the incident to school authority to prevent the situation from escalating.

(3) *Facebook screenshot of a conversation between Daniel and Harrison Oh (Page 14).*
Whoever presented this evidence was obviously want to frame a case to incriminate Daniel, and as a result will have a lot explanation to do. The screenshot was carefully framed so that it looks like Daniel started the dialogue and also said the last sentence. In reality, this dialogue occurred on Robin

Zhang's Facebook status. Robin Zhang made a joke toward Daniel; then Harrison Oh insulted Daniel in the following comment. Another student also joined the conversation, and Daniel was actually the 4th people joined the conversation. At the end, there are also three sentences that were cut off. By cutting off both ends, it looks like Daniel started and ended the dialogue. In reality, Harrison Oh started the exchange by insulting Daniel and said the last words.

On Friday, April 2nd, 2010, Mrs. Bush showed Daniel a Facebook printout to accuse him of cyber bullying Harrison Oh. Daniel wanted to examine that evidence but Mrs. Bush refused to allow him to even have a close look. In his statement to Mr. Fahge, Daniel challenged that evidence and specifically asked for a copy of that color printout. However, the school never responded. Daniel believes the color copy Mrs. Bush briefly showed to him on April 2nd, 2010 was the same conversation between him and Harrison Oh but was altered by removing most of Harrison Oh's comments.

It is obvious to us that somebody made an effort to bully and humiliate Daniel by gaming the system. We would not make a great deal of such action if this was just a trick played by a teenage since as a minor he might have limited understanding of potential damage and consequences of such action. What troubled us was the fact that the school used such tempered document to punish Daniel, even after Daniel challenged it. If the school continues to accuse Daniel of cyber-bullying based on such tempered document, we will have to request a formal investigation on this unethical and even fraudulent act.

(4) *The printout from Twitter*

Although not mentioned in the official suspension notice, in Mr. Fahge's email on April 5th, 2010 "involvement in temporary theft of Fred Guo's headphone" was cited (See Attachment 1). The only evidence school relied on to make such accusation was a printout of Twitter input nine month ago. The school's use of web based information that is nine months old to insinuate Daniel has a penchant for stealing headphones is outrageous. Daniel never stole Fred's cell phone or headphones. We noticed that Twitter printout was not included in the document you sent to us, but we still believe the school owes Daniel at least an explanation why such evidence was collected and used in the first place.

2. **The suspension is not reasonable.**

The whole process started with a conflict between George Tang and Fred Guo over Fred Guo's phone being taken and ended up with Daniel being physically assaulted by Fred Guo. During this process, Daniel did not take Fred Guo's phone or headphones, was a victim of physical assault by Fred Guo, reported the incident to school authorities to prevent the situation from escalating, and then was punished more than the people who committed assault and battery. Any logic behind such decision will not survive even the most cursory scrutiny.

The school's decision to suspend a student who was the victim of physical assault and properly reported the incident has created a negative incentive not only for our son but for all students regarding reporting of assaults on school grounds, which will in turn lead to an unsafe, both physically and psychologically, learning environment at school. The impact of that negative incentive cannot be overstated.

3. **It was unfair and it was not evenhanded.**
   Daniel was physically assaulted by another student during school hour while on school grounds, did not fight back and reported the incident. Even a causal inquiry of US tort law would lead to an obvious conclusion that the other student committed assault and battery against Daniel. Equally clear is the school police which specifies that the disciplinary action for such offense is five day suspension and a policy report. However, the school made the decision to suspend the student who committed assault and battery for one days while to suspend Daniel for two days. The accusation of Daniel being provocative is legally meaningless, preposterous, and simply a red herring, because the law specifically excludes provocation as a defense of assault and battery.

   The school appeared oblivious to both the factual and indisputable violent act and the school policy when handling the offense by the other student. On the other hand, the school used web-based information that is highly disputable and unclear policy to impose a heavier punishment on Daniel. By adopting such double standard and applying school policy inconsistently, the school damns itself both ways. It invites challenges to the rationale of the suspension decision. And it calls attention to the professionalism and ethicality demonstrated during the investigation and decision making process.

4. ***The school did not follow proper procedure to reach the suspension decision***

After Daniel reported that he was physically assaulted by Fred Guo on Thursday, April 1st, 2010 and before the suspension decision was made on Friday April 2nd, 2010, school authorities claimed that they spent significant time and efforts to investigate the incident and interviewed at least 10 people. During this process school authorities prepared new allegations and gathered evidence against Daniel but never interviewed Daniel and never gave him an effective opportunity to defend himself.

In his email on April 6th, 2010 (See Attachment 2) Mr. Fahge claimed "at least 4 different opportunities". However, such claim is palpably inaccurate. The so-called first opportunity is when Daniel reported that he was physically assaulted. At that time, Daniel had no idea that the school was going to accuse him of "behavior leading to a fight" and "cyber-bullying of another student". It is clear this was not an opportunity for Daniel to defend himself or present any evidence. The so-called 3rd and 4th opportunities never actually occurred and only became a topic of discussion after the suspension decision was made and Daniel had challenged the decision.

Only the second one, i.e. the meeting with Mrs. Bush on Friday, April 2nd, 2010 could be an opportunity for Daniel, but unfortunately it was not. In the same email, Mr. Fahge provided Mrs. Bush's account about the meeting (the first paragraph). Daniel believes that paragraph is not an accurate description of what happen. Here we just want to point out an obvious error: the 6th period ends at 2:12pm, and therefore it is impossible for the meeting to take place "around 2:00 pm". This may seem to be a minor detail, however, the error on this simple and easy-to-check fact casts doubt about the rest of the description.

Through a little careful examination of this paragraph we can find:

- *Daniel was accused of being "defensive", indicating the purpose of this meeting was not for him to defend himself;*
- *The conversation was described as being "unproductive", indicating this meeting did not effectively serve the purpose of providing Daniel an opportunity to defend himself.*
- *If the goal of the first part of the meeting was to give Daniel a chance to present his point of view or to collect additional information to make the final decision and the conversation was "unproductive", it is clear that suspension decision was made based on partial information.*

Therefore, this meeting was not intended to be and did not serve the purpose of providing an opportunity for Daniel to defend himself, as required by California Education Code (48911 (b)) and school district policy. School's failure to afford Daniel a due process also undermined the constitutional right of Daniel.

5. **Some practices demonstrated by school officials are at least unprofessional.**
   We were deeply troubled by not only the suspension decision but also the practices and conducts demonstrated during the process. Here we just list a few examples:

   (1) *Distorting facts.*
   Defining what happened on April 1ˢᵗ, 2010 as "physical altercation" (See Attachment 1) is profoundly misleading. The undisputable fact is that Fred Guo committed assault and battery toward Daniel.

   (2) *Claimed to have given multiple opportunities for Daniel to present his statements although the truth is that after Daniel reported the physical assault and battery committed by Fred Guo and before the suspension was made, the school authority never interviewed Daniel and never gave him a chance to defend himself.*

   (3) *Using irrelevant documents as evidences:*
   - *A printout from Urbandictionary.com that was showed to Daniel by Mrs. Bush to accused him of being saying bad words toward to Coach James Bake. Daniel has nothing to do with that document.*
   - *A printout from Twitter to accuse Daniel of stealing Fred Guo's headphone.*

(4) *Using tempered document as evidence (See above about Facebook screenshot used to accuse Daniel of cyber-bullying Harrison Oh).*

(5) *Repeatedly ignoring parents request for information and failing to directly respond to our concerns.*

Such conducts, especially the conduct of using irrelevant and tempered documents to make the accusation, are extremely troubling. They are at least unprofessional, and in contradictory to the fundamental ideas of fairness, due process, equal justice that we cherish so much this land. If not challenged, such behaviors would create a hostile environment at school and jeopardize equal educational opportunity as guaranteed by the California Constitution and the United States Constitution. Daniel would be living in constant fears if he could be accused and punished at any time by the school using evidences randomly picked from somewhere. It is very difficult to resist to ask: why the student who is prima facie responsible for physical assault and battery was not disciplined based on school policy and the law? Why did the school quickly shift its attention from the student who committed assault and battery to the victim of such violent act? Why did the school cheery pick a few pieces of information from online activities occurred over more than one year period to cobble together an accusation against Daniel who is a victim of the physical assault? Why did the school rush to a decision to punish Daniel without giving Daniel a chance to defend himself as required by the law?

In summary, the suspension decision was not made based on facts or evidences, inconsistent with California

Education Codes or school district policies, unreasonable, and unfair. The school did not follow proper procedure to conduct the investigation and make the decision. Therefore we respectively ask you to remove the suspension from Daniel's school record.

This incident had and continues to have profound impact on Daniel. We will appreciate if you could expedite your investigation so that this matter could be satisfactorily resolved as soon as possible. We hope eventually we make this incident a positive learning experience for Daniel so that he can believe in the fundamental ideas of fairness, due process and equal justice in this land.

In the event that you do not agree with our request we would like to know what the process is for an appeal to the next level.

Very truly yours,

Michael Liu and Anna Liu

Chapter Seventeen

THING DIED DOWN for awhile. I began to focus more on the AP Tests and SAT II tests coming up. I began to practice violin vigorously for an upcoming audition I had. Life at school also returned back to normal for me. The principal never had another meeting with my parents.

Summer came.

I was at home with my grandparents during the first week of the summer when the house phone rang.

"Get ready. We have a meeting with the superintendent today in about an hour," my mom said.

My mom picked me up at my house and took me to the school district's office, which had relocated to what looked to be temporary housing.

On the way there, my mom gave me advice on how to talk and what to emphasize when talking to the superintendent. This was probably my last chance to make a lasting impression and get the suspension appealed.

My dad also drove there and the three of us got there a few minutes before the offices even opened. We saw a lady park a car close to us, get out and walk into the office. She must be the secretary.

When it was finally time for our appointment, we got out of the car and walked into the trailer like building.

"Hi," said the secretary that just walked in, "How can I help you?"

"We have a 10:30am appointment with Superintendent Anderson," my dad said.

"Oh yes, I will go tell her that you're here. Please have a seat," she said.

Five minutes later, I was sitting at a table with the superintendent, my mom, and my dad.

"Thanks for coming. I have reviewed the case. First of all I had to say there were a lot of errors on the official suspension notice, and I believe the unnecessary linking of what happened on April 1st and the online activities that happened some time ago caused a lot of confusion. However, I had to say the some of what Daniel said online was not appropriate, and I believe the one day suspension is justified but the school has to make the correction of the suspension notice. Those online activities have nothing to do with what happened on April 1st." Said the Superintendent to open up the discussion.

"I know you do not live in Chester but you have all proper paper to be in Chester schools. He is an excellent student, isn't it?" She said.

"Probably not by parent standards." My dad with a smile.

"So personally I want him to graduate from Chester high." She said, obviously trying to convey a message that we do not need to fight for the suspension due to the fear that I would not be able to stay in Chester high.

"Thanks, but whether he can stay at Chester high is not our concern right now." My dad said.

"Any suspension will be in his student record, but it is confidential and we will not disclose it to anybody unless this is court order, and it will not be included in the transcript. After he graduated the record will just threaded. So it won't have impact on his college applications." She added.

"We knew that, so the impact on college applications is not the reason that we want to appeal the suspension." My mom said.

"We want to appeal this suspension because it is unfair. Right now what we are most concerned is the impact of this unfair treatment on Daniel. As parent, we want him to finish high school as Chester and we definitely care which college he can go to, but those are not the main reason that we want to appeal." My dad said very passionately.

The superintendent turned to me, "I do want to hear from you what do you think."

"I know I did stupid thing online, but I don't think I cyber bully anybody. If you think I was cyberbullying based on those evidence, then you have to suspend at least 90% of school students." I answered.

"Why it seems there is so much hate in the online communications with Harrison?"

"I don't think that is hatred. Most kids say stupid thing online." I answered.

"How would describe your relationship with Harrison?"

"He is not my friend but I won't say I hate him".

"I am going to ask the school to provide consoling to you and other students that involved in this incident to learn how to treat each other."

"He has been already under psychological therapy for some time." My dad said.

"Oh," she seems a little surprised.

"As we mentioned in the letter to you, this incident has significant impact on him, that is also why on that Monday I tried so hard to ask the school to postpone the suspension so that we could have more time to understand the situation. As parents we tried to work with school to manage the situation, and we have to seek professional help." My dad said.

Then she started to ask me about how I felt.

Finally someone was actually willing to listen to what I had to say, what I wanted to say.

"I don't feel safe at school," I said simply.

"Really?" she asked, "Can you describe it more?"

"I mean, I'm not scared that someone is going to shoot me in the face when I walk into class. I'm actually not scared of any of the students that much. I'm not scared that Fred or Harrison would bully me or anything. I'm more scared of the school. I feel bullied by the school," I said.

The superintendent did not respond immediately.

"So you feel more threatened by the school than by any students," she repeated.

"Yes, I have no trust in that the school will be there to protect me or help me if I need help," I said.

"What can we do to change that?" she asked.

"I don't think you can," I said.

"Do you still have friends at school?" she asked.

"Yes, a lot of friends," I said.

"What are their names?" she asked.

"Everybody is my friend," I said.

"But who are your best friends?"

"Everybody," I said again.

"I think this is what he has learned too," my mom said with a smile.

"Yes, he's not naming any specific names anymore, why's that?" Mrs. Anderson asked me.

"I don't trust you, frankly. I'm afraid that if I tell you specific names that you will go question them. And I'm not going to let you do that," I said.

"So you have trust issues," she said.

"Absolutely," I said.

"If you don't feel safe at the school or you don't like to school anymore, why do you want to stay? You now live in Richland, you can go to Nuder High School. It's a great school." She said.

I looked at her, and said "I do not want to run away."

"But we want you to feel welcomed and happy at the school. Did anybody bother you at school?" She asked.

"Nobody can bother me now." I answered.

"What if somebody says something that you don't like?" She asked.

"I just ignore them." I answered.

"Can you give me an example?" She asked.

"Harrison tried to pick on me at least two times." I said.

"What did he do?" She asked.

"One time was during lunch he could not find his necklace and I was sitting two people away from him. He asked me whether I took it. I told him 'No', and then he said' Daniel, you just recently be suspend, if I reported this you will be in big trouble.' Well, I didn't have it, and you can do whatever you want to do." I said.

"Did this bother you or make you feel angry or anything?" She asked.

"No.' I answered. "It didn't bother me. What he said means nothing to me. I just ignored him."

The superintendent looked at me, and said "This is a very unhealthy situation. That is also why we take the cyberbully issue so seriously."

"But what the school did to Daniel actually helped to create such a hostile environment at school." My dad said. "This is also the first time we heard what Harrison did. The school accused Daniel of cyberbullying Harrison. The evidence, which I assume is provided by Harrison, is the online communication between him and Daniel. However, that screenshot was carefully framed by cutting off both ends so that it looks like Daniel started the conversation and said the last words. In reality, he first insulted Daniel and said the last words. In fact, Daniel believed that the evidence Mrs. Bush showed him on that Friday was different from the one you provided. In that color copy most of Harrison's comments was removed so it looks like a monologue by Daniel. Daniel had challenged that evidences but the school never listened to Daniel and even after he challenged never respond, instead insisted to use that tempered evidence against Daniel. Now you see Harrison feels empowered and keep bullying Daniel at school." When talking about this, my dad became very emotional.

"But the school has to take cyberbullying seriously." The Superintendent said.

"We have no problem with that. But the school needs to be fair and follow the rules. On one hand the school use irrelevant and even fraudulent online information to punish Daniel, but on the other hand did not follow the clear rule to punish Fred Guo? It is stated very clearly that it should be five days suspension and a police report." My dad said.

"Not necessarily five days, it's a range." The superintendent argued.

"No. For assault and battery there is a five day suspension and police report. We studied the law, we have consulted multiple lawyers, and we even consulted the police department, it's no question that Fred committed assault and battery against Daniel. He hit Daniel and Daniel did not fight back. So it was not a fight, it was assault and battery, and we could press charges against him. What Daniel said before is not relevant since provocation is not a defense of assault and battery. It is very clear to us that the school did not follow its own rule when handling the offense committed by Fred Guo. But as I said many times, we had no interested in how you educate the other kid, that should be between the school and his parents. All we want is a fair treatment of our son." My dad became very emotional. "So we never asked how many days Fred was suspended."

"You should not ask and we cannot disclosed that information." The superintendent chipped in.

"But do you know how we figured out? Fred hit Daniel on Thursday, Mrs. Bush met with Daniel on Friday to accuse him, and Monday evening Daniel received a threat from the Tennis team coach. Why? Because Fred's mom spread the rumor that Daniel said bad words about the coach during the tennis practice. So we knew Fred was suspended for only one day since he was at the tennis practice. The evidence used to accuse Daniel saying bad words against the tennis coach was a printout from Urbandictionary that Daniel has nothing to do with.

How come Mrs. Bush used that evidence on Friday and on Monday Fred's mom spread the false information if the school was so diligent in keeping all the disciplinary information confidential?" My dad' voice was quivering and his hand was shaking.

"So you think the school favors Fred." The superintendent said.

"It seems very obvious to us."

"But why is that?" The superintendent asked.

"That is the question we would like to have an answer to." My dad said.

"I don't have an answer, what's your opinion?" The superintendent asked again.

"Well, we do not want to speculate, but we do know the Fred's father used to be teacher at Chester High. Anyway, we would rather focus our conversation on whether you think the punishment to Daniel is fair based on the evidence the school presented."

The details of the discussion after that are unimportant. But after much back and forth, she finally changed her mind and agreed that if I stayed out of trouble the first semester of my senior year, that she would completely erase the suspension from my record.

AT THE END of the meeting, she gave me some advice. The one I remember most clearly is: *advocate for yourself.* To me that not only meant when I was facing trouble, but on a daily basis to be a first rate version of myself. In that way I am also advocating for myself because if I do nothing wrong, I would not have to back off from anybody.

I guess I did learn a few things from this interesting journey. I'll probably be more careful of what I say or type.

I'll probably watch and see who I can trust to keep my words to themselves. But the biggest thing that changed is that I simply don't trust people anymore.

> *When you want to test the depths of a stream, don't use both feet—Confucius.*

That pretty much summarizes my new attitude during social interactions now. I'm glad I got through and was successful in appealing the suspension. But I'm not proud that I live and attend a school that was so eager to suspend me. I'm not proud that the school's system of punishing its students is totally different from the legal system of the United States of America. Instead of innocent until proven guilty, students are guilty until proven innocent.

Well, at least in Chester, California.

Epilogue

Although Ms. Bush and Mr. Fahge thought that they were acting in compliance to school policy when they made the decision to suspend me, their attitude toward me throughout the ordeal made the matter personal. It just seemed like when my parents and I decided to appeal the suspension, they took it as a question of their intelligence and/or judgment when all we wanted was to point out that they missed some key information and evidence along the way. We just wanted to show them that if they listened to us the way they listened to Harrison and Fred they would find that their reason for suspending me was wrong.

Their decision was made before I had a chance to speak to them. And when I did present my case, I was shot down when they told me what I said meant nothing anymore. It was like I was the villain for even daring to plead my case, a chance I should have gotten in the first place.

For the rest of junior year, I kept a low profile and felt paranoid about everything I said. I was able to make it through the year by just maintaining a good friendship with my close friends and avoiding anything that could lead to trouble. All I had to do was graduate and go to college, I thought, then I can leave this place forever.

So I stayed out of trouble the first semester of my senior year and the suspension was removed from my record just in time for college admissions. But for how long and hard I had to fight for it and the toll it took on me, getting it removed from my record was hardly a reward. But I got over it because I believe that what I got from the whole process is not nearly as important as what I learned from the process.

By the end of senior year, things were pretty much back to the way they were. I had been able to move on from the fiasco of the previous year. I played tennis again and had redeveloped a friendly relationship with tennis coach James Bake. It was the best year of tennis I had ever been a part of and we had our best season ever. But there was still no denying the effect that my suspension had on me. I learned to be a nicer person, got in good graces with some friends I had alienated before, and kept controversial opinions to myself. Senior year flew by and though I had my share of difficulties, I was more than ready to get out of Chester High.

About a week before graduation, our school held an awards ceremony for the seniors. I wasn't the greatest student out there, but I was up for a couple of awards. One required me to walk up to the front and shake Ms. Bush's hands. It was an award only about ten people in the entire senior class won and one that took some intelligence to win. As I shook Ms. Bush's hand, she seemed surprised that I was capable of winning such an award. But I wasn't surprised she saw me as a dumb troublemaker. And I looked her right in the eye as if to say: that's right you really don't know me at all.